GRIFT

A TWISTY CON-ARTIST CAPER

RL DONOVAN

EDGE HOUSE PRESS

1

———————

"I'm choking."

"Then take off the damn tie, James."

The tie slid through his collar and onto the couch like a red serpent awaiting its prey. He trudged to the fridge, grabbed a pale ale labeled Devil's Brew and banged the neck against the counter. "That's better." He gulped the beer and smacked his lips.

He leaned over the counter. "Who's our mark?"

"You must be patient. I'll tell you soon. Promise." Shanice replaced her tea at the precise center of the glass coaster. Absently, she flipped through *Real Estate Today*, not looking up at him.

James shrugged and plopped down on the slippery black leather couch. "I only ask because I can't take this straight job thing much longer. I did that for twenty years, remember?"

"No one loves a pity party." She still stared at her magazine. But the corner of her mouth lifted in a smile.

"Those guys at the office, they're just brutal." He took another swig of beer. "You know what they did today? They told me to review accounts for the last twenty-five years."

"Sounds fascinating." Shanice edged the magazine to the middle of the coffee table. She leaned back and surveyed James. "But hey—you signed up for this glamorous life, didn't you?"

A scraping sound came at the front door, followed by a clunk. "I'm home, honeys!" giggled a voice from the entryway.

"Ta-da!" A petite figure in tulle and ballet shoes waltzed into the room. Daisy chains draped over her long twists, which twirled as she spun around. To complete her entrance, she tiptoed into the center of the room and lowered herself into the splits.

"What the hell are you doing, Nia?" James spilled the rest of the beer on his shirt.

Shanice chuckled. "Looks like you've had an accident." She offered him a napkin.

He rubbed his shirt with the napkin, which only made the stain spread. "Can we switch jobs? Yours seems more fun than mine." He wrinkled his nose at the sour smell of the beer.

"Can you do the splits?" Nia's daisy chains slipped onto the floor. Still in her impossible position, she scooped up the flowers and wound them twice around her wrist.

"OK, but, no, seriously, what are you doing?"

She gracefully lifted herself from the floor. "Well, I used to be a ballerina—I trained from childhood through college." She floated onto the sofa and stared wistfully out of the bay window. "But then life got in the way."

"So this is a new hobby?"

Shanice intervened. "No, I asked her to restart her lessons. I see she's totally immersed herself in the role. Better get changed, Nia." Shanice stared at her phone.

James threw his head back into the cushions. "Where are we going now?"

"To meet a thief."

———

"ARE WE GOING TO A RESTAURANT?" James ambled down the front steps of the blue-and-purple Georgian house. It had been a real find. Fit their purpose perfectly—a quiet neighborhood where everyone kept to themselves. And its location in Mill Valley, one of the most expensive towns on earth, wasn't too bad either. No cops prowling around.

"No, we've got to go to Sonoma." Shanice opened the burgundy RAV4's front door.

"But that will take hours!" protested Nia, now clad in jeans and a T-shirt.

"Does it help if we're going to a winery?" Shanice buckled up.

"Marginally." James slid on his sunglasses. He used the sunglasses as a shield to watch Shanice. For a split second, he felt a twinge of guilt about staring at her like this, but he rarely got the chance. Her open, round face told him nothing. She had the best poker face he'd ever seen. And she couldn't hide behind her hair as it was closely cropped, though she did always wear a figure-concealing, drapey long cardigan. Small shell earrings swung gently as she adjusted the rearview mirror, but nothing else moved. Until she stuck the keys into the ignition. Her hand quivered, ever so slightly.

Nia tapped him on the shoulder. "Dear DJ, would you put on our playlist?"

Nodding, James connected his phone to the car speakers. They all agreed the best way to survive car trips over the next few months would be alternating genre playlists. Shanice and Nia submitted their choices to James. Shanice preferred really old-school R&B. When Nia had asked about nineties artists, Shanice had told her she meant the sixties and seventies.

Nia enjoyed country. And to Nia and Shanice's everlasting chagrin, James preferred soft rock. While he could understand why it wasn't their favorite, he couldn't understand why they were irritated by it.

Otis Redding switched to Charlie Parker. They all enjoyed jazz, so every fourth playlist song provided a musical pause.

The golden hills of Novato whipped past

them as they drove north on Highway 101. James turned up the volume as the traffic slowed, just to annoy the other cars. Uptight, selfish Marinites. Hell, he was one himself.

"Do we have anything to eat?" Nia whined from the backseat.

Her simple question threw James back in time, a time that seemed an age ago. One where he had sat with his wife, Alana, traveling to Oregon, with their daughter, Katrina, in the backseat. She was forever asking for food. They had been good times. So why did his chest tighten at the memory?

"James? Hello? Are you there?" Shanice slid her sunglasses halfway down her nose. "I put some nuts in the glove compartment."

James clicked it open. Amid the neatly stacked papers, he spotted two plastic bags filled with nuts. He swiped the large bag of almonds and tossed it to Nia.

As he looked back at the half-empty space, the late-afternoon sun hit something shiny and metallic.

A gun.

2

———————

"Keep your pants on." Shanice leaned over and shut the glove compartment.

"You said no violence." Sweat trickled from the nape of his neck.

"And there won't be." Shanice shifted gears as they came to another traffic standstill. She lifted her sunglasses and waved her hand at the glove compartment. "Really. It's just in case."

James rubbed his brow. "I don't know. Maybe this is all a mistake."

"Oh no, Mr. Ambrose." Shanice shook her head and clenched her jaw. "You said you were in. Why this sudden change of heart?"

Ambrose. His new last name. When he didn't have to use his old name, Bowman, that is.

"I dunno," James mumbled in reply. Why was he getting cold feet? He didn't even know what to worry about. All he knew was he had to keep that ridiculous job. It shouldn't be too hard.

Shanice locked both arms straight on the wheel as she navigated a sharp curve. "I'll tell you why you're nervous. Do you want me to tell you why you're nervous? You can't get mad at me for speaking the truth."

His gut told him he didn't want to know, but he said, "Go on, I can handle it."

"Because you're used to being where I am all the time—in the driver's seat. That's been your whole life, hasn't it?" She smirked.

"Well, I suppose when you put it like that . . ." he trailed off.

"There is no 'putting it like that'—I'll admit it myself. If I were a middle-aged white man—instead of an almost-middle-aged Black woman—used to calling the shots and that was all I knew, I'd be scared shitless, too."

James said nothing but gave the slightest

nod. He wrinkled his nose and closed the window. It smelled like they were getting near one of the oil refineries.

"Here endeth the first lesson," she said, and laughed. "I'm only telling you because I have to. Otherwise, I'd keep my mouth shut."

"Thanks," he mumbled. She was right. He turned to Nia. "Am I really so transparent?"

Nia nearly choked on her almonds.

Peals of laughter filled the car.

———

THE RAV4 TRUNDLED over potholes on a pockmarked dirt road. The golden hills looked practically alight from the twilight glow, though the occasional cloud of dust obscured them as they rolled over a large hole.

A growling noise echoed inside the car. Or was it outside the car?

"Sorry!" Nia flopped around in the back-seat like a freshly caught trout. "My stomach. Can we have real dinner when this is over?"

Ignoring Nia, Shanice said, "How far are we supposed to go along this road?"

James peered down at his phone. "The turnoff should've been point-three miles ago. Damn GPS maps." He shook his phone. "Shit. I lost the signal."

"You didn't save a PDF of the map?" Nia leaned forward.

"No, I didn't save a PDF of the map," he parroted.

"I see someone else besides me is hungry," said Nia.

He shrugged. "I guess we'll have to just look for a *Ghost Town Winery* sign."

"What kind of name is that?" asked Nia.

"One that doesn't want too many visitors," deadpanned Shanice.

"There it is!" yelped Nia. "On the right."

As the dust settled, a hand-carved sign greeted them. A little Casper-the-ghost perched on top, pointing to the right. The sign artist had missed the mark, thought James. The ghost had a sinister smirk rather than a friendly smile.

In the rearview mirror, he saw Nia shudder. "Ah, can you say 'creepy'?" she whispered, hunching over toward the two in the front seat.

"Shhh." Shanice held a finger to her lips.

The engine pinged as the car cooled. Oak-tree branches rustled over the sign.

"What's the drill?" James whispered.

A great scratching, screeching noise pierced the silence.

3

———————

Nia's long fingernails sunk into James' shoulder.

He clamped his hand over hers, willing her to stop. "It's OK, it's OK." He squinted at the German Shepherd's black snout tapping at the window. "It's just a dog scratching the car."

Shanice gripped the wheel. "Get that damn dog off my car, James."

"Drive on slowly and it should leave us alone."

She shifted into gear and maneuvered around the next pothole.

"The dog is gone." James watched the

perplexed animal amble after them in the rearview mirror.

Shanice wiped her forehead with a handkerchief. Despite the situation, James smiled to himself—who else but Shanice would carry a handkerchief?

"OK, thanks for your patience. Here's the plan. Just follow my lead. We're meeting an old friend of mine named Edie."

"She's the thief?" asked Nia.

"Don't tell her, but yes, she's the thief."

"Why do I have the feeling something's not right here?" Nia tapped on her window.

"Because it's not. Your instincts are on point. Follow me."

James surveyed the winery. He didn't think they'd had a guest since the first Bush administration. Grapevines dotted the landscape, but many had shriveled or retreated toward the earth. A rusty tractor sat near an equally rust-colored barn. The doors to the barn swung on their half-dislodged hinges, revealing decaying haybales inside. He wrinkled his nose. Moldy hay.

A white cat scuttled across the dirt pathway up to the main house. The lawn—if one could call it that—looked like a balding man's head with a bad haircut.

Nia and James huddled together on the pathway. Their backs faced one another, readying for an attack. The cat sat near them, licking its paw. At least the cat seemed oblivious to the atmosphere.

Shanice waved them on toward the front porch. Then she waved again so hard James was sure she'd dislocate her shoulder.

Ah well, he thought. All part of the plan, right? Trust the plan, James, trust the plan.

The screen door creaked open.

Tap, tap.

Knock, knock.

Thump. Thump.

"Edie, are you in there?" Shanice stuck her ear against the door.

Shuffling footsteps approached. Someone muttered as they disengaged an elaborate lock system.

A white woman with washed-out blond hair popped around the doorframe. Her eyes slewed from Shanice, to James, and to Nia.

The door flung open. "Come in, but be extra quiet. I don't want to disturb Dan."

"Why, is he sleeping?" hissed Nia.

"No, but he has supersonic hearing—he's pottering around in the barn."

"Will he be upset we're here?"

All three women glared at James. He held his hands up in mock surrender.

"Have a seat," whispered Edie. "I'll get my stuff. Be back in a minute."

James looked around in mild disgust. Clothes and magazines mushroomed over a stained plaid couch. Vinyl wood-paneled walls had a yellow tinge, probably because they hadn't been washed since they were installed in the seventies. A lone oil painting of a tiny cabin in the woods adorned the wall. Takeout boxes and microwave dinner trays littered the coffee table. And the stench. Dead rat?

Nia pinched her nose and waved a hand. "What's that smell?!" The windows and glass doors were shut. Nia marched over and promptly opened them. "Ah." A welcome breeze rescued their olfactory senses. "So much better."

"What are you doing?" hissed Edie from the stairway. "Close the door! Dan will hear us. Please."

Wrinkling her nose in distaste, Nia did as

she was told.

Edie disappeared and then returned a minute later to lean over the banister. "If Dan comes, go to the car and start it."

Shanice held up a thumb.

"Can't we just get in the car? I don't want to meet this Dan character." Nia shifted from side to side.

"But I'd like to meet you."

The trio spun around. The thin white man in overalls looked like someone out of *The Grapes of Wrath*—complete with red suspenders—; not the hipster kind, either. What hair remained on his pasty head was arranged in a greasy combover. James thought it unfortunate the man hadn't been clued into the shaving-your-head trend. Though he was rail-thin, muscles strained through the missing buttons on his shirt.

They all knew what to do.

A car revved its engine outside.

Edie slid down the banister with a large duffel bag in one hand and a purse around her shoulder. Dodging her husband, she ran toward the front door. Nia and James tore off after her and let the screen door bang shut.

And then James tripped over the cat.

"Meeooww . . . skiissssh." The cat scratched at his jeans.

Dan was on the front porch, flashing a piece of metal. Shit.

James lifted himself to his feet and rushed toward the car. The cat's claws hung on to his jeans. He dragged the cat to the car, with the cat protesting all the way.

He leapt into the open car door, the cat following him unwillingly.

"Edie!" Dan leveled the gun at the car. "Come back here. Now."

"Meeeoooww!"

The door stood open as James scrambled to remove the cat.

Edie already had the car shifted into reverse so they drifted backward and then gained momentum as Dan moved toward the car. Shanice had bent her head down, as had Nia. James did too, but he had to detach the cat.

As they picked up speed, James gave up and slammed the door, cat still attached to his leg.

A shot rang out.

4

———

The bullet pinged and ricocheted off the car roof.

Dust clouds ballooned as they sped in reverse up the driveway. At the top of the hill, the dust settled. Dan trudged up behind them with a robotic step.

"Go, go, go!" yelled Edie.

"I am!" Shanice hit the gas pedal.

"Meooow!" screeched the cat.

Though the car limped through the potholes, they soon arrived at the main road. James craned his neck. "Terminator is nowhere in sight. We can all breathe now."

A collective sigh filled the air. As if on

cue, the cat purred, cozily ensconced between Nia and James.

Silence reigned until the freeway entrance loomed in the distance. Nia burst out,
"I'm Nia, Edie. Nice to meet you. What the
fuck is wrong with your husband?"

"Oh, Dan, he's harmless, really. Just talks
a big game."

"Sorry, Edie—I'm James, by the way—but
pointing a gun at us is more than a game."

Shanice shifted gears. "First, your damn
dog scratched my car and then your de-
ranged husband dinged up the frame. You're
better off without that joker."

Edie's body crumpled. She sobbed.
Without missing a beat, Shanice deftly
swiped a packet of tissues from the side
pocket and handed it to Edie.

Shanice exited the freeway and wound
around to a small Thai restaurant. "C'mon.
Let's eat. There's no point in talking till we've
filled our bellies."

Nia and James looked at the cat. "Edie,"
said Nia, "what should we do with your cat?"

"What? Oh." She twisted around. "That's
Opal. Glad she'll be joining us."

James wasn't so sure. His first encounter with Opal had been less than satisfactory.

"Ah, yes, Edie," cooed Nia. "But what should we do with Opal while we're in the restaurant?"

"She's a good kitty. We can leave the windows open a crack and bring her back a few scraps from dinner. We shouldn't be too long."

Nia and James shrugged, patted the cat, and inhaled the savory smell wafting out of the restaurant.

———

THE PAD THAI WAS SWEET, but not too sweet.

Nia scrunched up her face. "This is missing something." She pointed her fork at the noodles in an accusatory manner. "I know. Not enough sugar."

James sighed, admiring Nia's lithe twenty-something frame. She ate anything with complete abandon. He glanced down at his growing middle-age paunch.

"Tastes just right to me." Shanice inserted a forkful of the quivering noodles into her mouth. "Why don't you order iced coffee or tea? The condensed milk will satisfy your sweet tooth."

"Yes! Great idea. Catch the server's eye, will you?"

Edie slid out of the booth and marched up to the server, then spun on her heel and turned back.

"Thanks, Edie," said Nia.

James set down his fork. Odd. Here was a woman who clearly took decisive action, yet she couldn't leave her pig of a husband.

The server arrived in a flash, with a highball glass of Thai iced tea. Nia sucked the orange liquid through a straw, stretched back in her chair and rubbed her stomach. "Much better. Let's head home—I'm all in."

Edie wriggled out of the booth again, leaving behind a half-eaten plate of chicken and vegetables. "I'll be back in a minute." She bobbed and weaved toward the restroom.

As soon as she was out of earshot, Nia leaned in.

"What is this all about? This crazy woman nearly gets us killed, then goes all white woman-weepy on us. And you say she's a thief?" Nia snorted.

Shanice shrugged. "You signed up to be part of a long con crew, Nia, and it takes all sorts to make up a decent crew. You know a white woman would have to go through hell and back with me in order for me to trust her."

"But you trust James," said Nia.

James waved his hand. "I am sitting at the table, in case you didn't notice."

Shanice chuckled. "James is a special case. Besides, I have no problem reading white men. What you see is what you get."

"Who's stereotyping now?" hissed James.

Shanice and Nia broke into laughter.

James' stomach clenched. His anger soon dissolved into puzzlement. Why were they laughing at him? Again? "Why am I such a joke to you two?"

Shanice wiped away a tear from her watering eyes. "Look. You wouldn't be here if we didn't trust you with a con. We wouldn't be poking fun at white people in front of you if we didn't trust you not to lash out."

Nia rolled her eyes.

James pointed at Nia. "See? She's rolling her eyes at me." He suddenly felt like he was an eight-year-old again, whining to his mother about his older sister. "Sorry. I know I'm being childish. I think it's hard because I have no idea what's going on. When are you going to tell us the plan?"

"It's true," said Nia. "I'm itching to get started."

"Here's your bill." The server slid the receipt tray onto the table, complete with four hard-candy mints. Nia pounced on a mint, popped it in her mouth, and sucked on it. James and Shanice pushed the remaining three toward her. Eyes alight, Nia threw them into her bag.

Shanice rummaged in her purse and pulled out a large zipped wallet. The credit card she put in the tray read *Charisse Miller*.

"Did you steal that?" whispered James.

Shanice's eyes flashed. "No, I did not steal it. I'm not a thief. How many times have I told you?"

"Tell you what?" Edie returned, refreshed and visibly less red-eyed.

"Nothing." Shanice gathered her purse on her lap. "By the way, Edie, I heard your phone blowing up while we were in the car. Can you put it in airplane mode? We don't want Dan tracking us down."

Edie laughed. "Dan couldn't find his way out of a paper bag."

For the first time—most likely because he wasn't preoccupied with his own physical safety—James noticed her voice had a slight twang in the way she said "bag." Arkansas? James had developed this hobby as a child when his family moved around a lot. US regional accents. It might come in handy. He didn't know how else he'd be useful on the team. He had deduced Shanice was from somewhere in the Midwest. Perhaps Chicago or St. Louis. And Nia was definitely from California. Most likely the Bay Area.

"Excuse me." James rose from the table. "I'll be back in a minute." He walked toward the bathroom. Once inside, he typed 'Charisse Miller" into Google. No luck. A gazillion Charisse Millers appeared. He clicked on "images" and scrolled through. He turned to leave, but then halted. There was a photo of Shanice, maybe ten years ago. He clicked on it and read the webpage. A newsletter dated 2010 said:

CHICAGO MEDICAL ASSOCIATION Newsletter

.   .   .

DR. CHARISSE MILLER, neurosurgeon at Chicago Harbor Hospital, named rising star for 2010 by the Chicago Medical Association. After completing her medical residency in 2007, Dr. Miller took a post at Chicago Harbor Hospital, where she specializes in comprehensive brain and spinal tumor surgery.

AND THAT WAS IT. No further explanation. His stubby fingers flew across the cramped phone keyboard, typing different combinations about neurosurgery and Charisse Miller, but the stories were all about her accomplishments. Nothing appeared after 2012.

It was as if she had vanished.

And in a manner of speaking, she had.

5

James' hand froze on the doorknob. The neighborhood, always a quiet one, was preternaturally quiet. Except for a determined solo cricket.

"Well, go on. Why are we waiting?" Nia moved closer to the door.

"The door was unlocked. I swore I locked it."

"You probably forgot." Nia pushed past him.

Shanice shunted her aside. "No. Better safe than dead. Let's go around to the kitchen." She waved them along. They wound around the side on a stone pathway lined with miniature trees. The smell of fresh wet earth revived him. A soft glow came from somewhere inside the house. Could be a flashlight. They filed up the rickety back stairs.

Shanice turned the lock, wincing as her fingers moved in slow motion.

They tiptoed through the kitchen toward the soft glow in the living room.

Despite his deteriorating eyesight, James saw a silhouette on the couch.

Shanice flicked the light switch.

"Miss Esme!" Nia sprinted toward an older woman in a raspberry-colored sleeveless dress. Noise-cancelling headphones that made her look like a child playing video games obscured her locs, styled as a bob. Nia nearly toppled over into her lap. Esme expertly pushed one ear cup to the side of her head and gave Shanice a bear hug. James thought he recognized the tinkling piano of Chopin. Nia gave her a peck on the cheek.

Shanice readjusted her drapey cardigan. "Miss Esme, what *are* you doing here? We weren't supposed to see you until tomorrow."

"Well, it was easier to escape the old folks home than I thought. The staff are not kind to Black folk and they think we've lost our marbles." She slipped off her headphones.

"So how'd you do it?" Nia nestled next to Esme on the couch.

Esme cocked her head and patted Nia's knee. "People are always coming and going in that place. You know, family, staff, new staff, and so on. What's the one thing they all have in common?"

"You know I love games, but not guessing games, Miss Esme," said Nia with a slight whine.

Esme held up her index finger in triumph. "Their one commonality is they're not old. Or at least not ancient like me."

James peered at Esme. Besides her salt-and-pepper hair, there was little about her that foretold her age. She might be anywhere from fifty to seventy.

Esme folded her hands in her lap. "So I used that to my advantage." She leaned over and pulled up a capacious Mary Poppins-style bag. After rummaging around, she pulled out a glossy, flat-hair wig. "I put this magical baby on and hey! I was forty again .. . OK, maybe fifty."

Nia put on the wig and grinned like a

goat in a briar patch, as James' grandmother used to say.

Esme smiled. "So after I got into character, I stuffed my things into this bag. Then I waited until lunchtime—when the staff serve food and visitors arrive. I simply strolled out the front door."

Shanice clapped and smiled. "Well done. But won't Shemekia and Anthony search for you?"

Esme shook her head and stared at her knees. "I'm sure the home will file a missing person's report, but I doubt Shemekia and Anthony will care. They'll probably be relieved." She clicked her tongue against her teeth.

Nia stroked Esme's shoulder. "Don't say that, Miss Esme. I'm sure your children love you."

Esme licked her lips. "Can we talk about something else, please? I'm just happy to see you all." She pulled a pair of glasses from her breast pocket, slid them onto her nose and peered at the crowd. "And who are these lovely people?" She gestured toward Edie and James.

Opal had slipped through Edie's arms

and sidled up to Esme on the couch. Esme patted the cat's head with one finger.

Edie scooped up the cat. "Oh, sorry." She offered one hand to Esme. "This is Opal. And I'm Edie. Pleased to meet you."

As they shook hands, Esme replied, "Pleased to meet you, and your cat. Though I'd prefer she not sit on me."

Edie looked affronted by the idea anyone wouldn't want a cat to crawl all over them. Nia intervened.

"Shanice has told me many stories about you." Nia bent over and squeezed Esme.

Shanice held up her hands and chuckled. "Not too much, don't worry, Miss Esme."

"And who is this charming man who looks like a . . ." Esme squeezed her eyes tight. "Don't tell me! A banker. No, a lawyer."

"Almost." James felt himself grin sheepishly. "A real estate broker."

"I was close!" She had a deep *heh-heh* gravelly laugh, the mark of a heavy smoker. Or perhaps a former heavy smoker.

"Pleased to meet you, Miss Esme. I'm James." He gripped her hand and was surprised by the strength of her grip in return.

Shanice stretched and yawned. "I'm sure

James will tell you all about why he's come over to join us, but he needs his beauty sleep before tomorrow."

"Why's that?" James brushed cat hair from his jacket.

"Because you're going to pass a test."

"Another test? Didn't I already pass enough tests?"

"But this one is a real one. An official test."

6

James turned over in his bed, sweating like a short-order cook. His gritty eyelids peeled back first toward the window, the crack in the ceiling, and then to the dreaded alarm clock. 5 a.m. He flopped over into a fetal position. Five more minutes.

He jolted upright as Opal's claws sunk into his flesh.

"Get off me!" he screeched, resisting the urge to fling the cat across the room. Instead, he pushed her away and groaned. 5:30. Time to get up if he didn't want to be late to the fucking exam.

Eyes still closed, he padded downstairs and into the kitchen.

"Esme!" Turning past the stove, he nearly toppled over the diminutive woman. "I'm so sorry," he mumbled, rubbing his eyes.

"Here you go, dear." She placed a cup of coffee in his hands. As his eyes seemed shut permanently, he was grateful.

"Oh—I—thank you." He slumped into a nearby barstool.

Within two minutes, the caffeine kicked in.

"What time did you get up, Miss Esme?" He popped a slice of bread in the toaster.

Esme's spoon clinked against her coffee mug. "Oh, round about four."

James crossed his arms. "I guess I have no excuse to be this tired at five-thirty."

"You're still young, you need your sleep."

He chuckled. "I wish. But I don't know what my excuse is at forty-five."

Esme bent her head over the kitchen island with a conspiratorial air. "Let me give you some advice, young man."

"About what?" He stopped munching on his toast slathered with butter. It slid onto the counter, narrowly missing the plate.

"About today. But not just today. I don't

know you but it looks like this is your usual routine to prepare for the workday, right?"

"Well, yes. Though it will be a shitty day."

She winced at his swearing. "Change your mindset and focus on your real job. When you're at a normal day job, you try to please your bosses or fight against them—sometimes both. But now none of that matters. Your real job is outside of all that. Everything you do from now on is part of the grift, you understand?"

James nodded and drained his third cup of coffee. "You mean it's like a conference? I'm there to get out of it whatever I can—I'm not there to ensure the conference runs smoothly."

Esme shifted on the stool, sipping her own coffee. "Well, yes. But grifting is more exciting." She smiled.

"Too right. A little too exciting this morning."

"You'd better take some tranquilizers if you think this is exciting, young man. Just you wait."

———

As THE BUS trundled over the Golden Gate Bridge, James' pulse quickened. The city view was one he never tired of, no matter what lay ahead that day. Somehow, the bridge made him feel special for just being on it as the steel cables whipped by, temporarily blocking the sparkle of the bay. Fog still draped over the city, but the weather report promised a hot day once the fog lifted. Beads of sweat rolled down his forehead in anticipation of being locked in a windowless human resources room.

"Your pants are buzzing." James' seatmate, clad in a purple tracksuit, turned away as if cell phones were a rather disgusting habit.

"Thanks—sorry about that." Maneuvering his large frame in the small seat, he finally retrieved his phone. He listened to the voicemail. "Hello, this message is for Mr. Bowman. This is Ruth Kettering calling from the City Planning Commission about the temporary position you applied for earlier this week. Please call me at your earliest convenience. Have a nice day."

As soon as the sour-smelling bus disgorged him at the human resources depart-ment, James returned the call.

"Hello. Yes, may I speak to Ruth Kettering? This is James Bowman, returning your call."

"Oh yes, Mr. Bowman. I'm calling with good news. We'd like to hire you for the temporary assistant position with the Planning Commission. Have you taken the Civil Service exam yet?"

"I'm about to take it."

"Well, you actually don't need to since it's a temporary position. You can take it later if it becomes a full-time position. We need you here as soon as possible."

James' shoulders dropped as he gesticulated wildly with his right hand. "Wonderful news. I don't suppose there's much to negotiate since it's a temp position, correct?"

"Correct, Mr. Bowman. Are you available to start today? We're only a ten-minute walk from human resources."

James gulped, but then remembered what Miss Esme had said this morning. "Yes, I'd be delighted. I'll come to your office."

He mouthed a little "Yes!" to himself. Shanice would be so impressed. He texted her, "I'm in at the planning commission. I can drop the other job." He, too, could be mysterious. This grifting business was a snap.

Were it not for his age and weight, he would have skipped down Market Street, gleefully tossing coins to everyone sitting on the sidewalk. His triumphant procession came to an abrupt halt as he nearly fell over a trash can. A black town car had pulled up to the curb. A long white leg peeked out from the car door. Then the rest of the body emerged. Her blond hair was pulled back in a fashionable bun, fairly glittering in the sunlight. She wore a cream-colored suit with modestly high red heels. And aviators. She looked cool, poised, and ready to run an obstacle course, finishing without a hair out of place or a spot on her suit.

Alana.

James' knees buckled as she entered the building opposite. It was DesignNiche, the rival developer firm to his own old firm, Tisdale Partners. A man in a similarly impeccable suit emerged. Not white, but impeccable nonetheless. Seth Hummel. Despite his five-thousand-dollar suit, he wore his sunglasses on the back of his head. A little tingle of satisfaction ran through James at this sight, but it was overwhelmed by an ocean of sadness. No, it wasn't sadness. It was jealousy and anger. If he were honest with himself, he wanted revenge. Revenge for ruining his life. He'd find a way. This was only the beginning. But the sadness returned when he thought of his daughter, Katrina.

The pair disappeared inside the building. He shook himself from his self-indulgent dreams of revenge.

Time to get to work.

7

——————

"So good to meet you, James." A tall, wiry man with a bald head as white as a cue ball shook his hand. "Fulton Girard."

"Mr. Girard, a pleasure. Thank you for this opportunity—I look forward to learning all about city government. Hope my experience in the private sector will prove useful."

"Undoubtedly." Fulton pulled back his lips, revealing pale gums. "Please, call me Fulton. And I've already heard the joke about Fulton Street. My family is from Jersey —my mother thought 'Fulton' made me sound important."

How was James supposed to reply? "Ah, yes, I'll call you Fulton."

Girard glanced at his phone. "Glad you could join us at such short notice. Your job application came in at a serendipitous moment. Though you're overqualified for the assistantship position, I couldn't pass up your connections."

"I'm new to all of this, but I'm not sure how I can use my connections inside government." Shanice told him to play the naïve fool for a while. It wasn't hard since he was clueless when it came to city government. Though he liked to think he wasn't a fool.

"Here, let's discuss this further before my next appointment." Girard waved James into his office, clapping him on the back in a time-honored masculine bonding ritual.

City government offices—at least at the planning department—were a step down from the cool, sleek surroundings of real estate developers' offices. It was a throwback to nineties' decor, thought James, looking at the large, droopy potted plant in the corner next to an ancient filing cabinet that probably hadn't been opened since the nineties.

Girard leaned back in his leather captain's chair and tapped a pen against his knee. "Close the door, would you?"

James sat in front of the massive gleaming oak desk.

Girard clicked his mouse while his eyes scanned the computer screen facing him. "So I understand your most recent job was with Tisdale Partners. You were there for five years. A long time. Why'd you leave?"

"Time to move on. I had hit a ceiling—not in terms of pay but in terms of challenge."

"I see that in the interview notes." Girard leaned back in his chair with his arms folded behind his head.

Power play position.

"I want to know why you *really* left TP. Full stop." Girard abandoned his power position as he leaned over the desk and brought his spiderlike fingertips together into a box formation. "I want your real answer."

James scratched his head. How should he play this? He couldn't go on with the country-boy attitude much longer if he wanted to be taken seriously by a planning commissioner.

The office smelled like the carpets hadn't been cleaned in at least ten years. He looked at the window with the hope it would magically open on its own. No chance. As he stared at the window sash, willing it to open, he noticed it had been painted shut.

"Well, Fulton." James did his best to lean back in his rather stiff wooden chair, mimicking Fulton's power pose. "I'll be honest, man to man." God. Had he really said 'man to man'? His new friends at home in Mill Valley would be appalled.

"It's true I wanted new challenges. But I'd also like to have my own firm someday—"

"I knew it." Girard cracked a satisfied smile.

"And to do it, I need to understand the planning—governmental process—better than I do. From the inside. That's why I've taken a substantial pay cut. And I've had personal challenges, which meant I needed a new direction in my life."

Whoops. Shouldn't have said that. But it was true.

"Hmmm . . . I see. Makes sense. You've come to the right place. I'll give you an insider's view." He paused for a sip of the green smoothie on his desk and then held up his index finger. "Though I expect reciprocity."

"What did you have in mind?"

"I want to know what goes on in developers' heads. I'm not from around here, so I need someone who can help me in that department. Catch my drift?"

James pursed his lips and nodded. "How about I set up informal gatherings? A lunch or dinner event. Casual. With my contacts. You can stop by since you're my new boss."

A light tap came from the door. A head popped around the opening.

"Mr. Girard, you'll be late to the commission meeting if you don't leave soon."

"Be right there, Marcy."

Girard turned back to James. "Marcy can show you to your desk. The hours here aren't hard, but I expect you to be more or less on call."

"Got it. And I'll set up a gathering soon. Maybe drinks? Or an informal get-together?"

"Sounds good."

"One more thing. I almost forgot." James pulled out a few slips of paper from his pocket. "I have two extra tickets to the ballet tonight. Box seats. My friends canceled, but I'm still going. Would you like them?"

Girard took the tickets and fanned the air with them. "Hmmm . . . well, as it happens, our plans fell through for tonight, so I'll see if my wife wants to go. Thanks." He slid them into a drawer.

"I'm sure you won't regret it."

8

———————

"You scrub up nice."

"C'mon, let's get on with it. No need to butter me up." Edie pushed a strand of hair behind her ear. Amazed by her transformation, James tried not to stare. When he had first seen her at her home, her hair had been limp and lifeless. Now it shone in a bell-like curve around her neck. And her face flushed with healthy color, set off by silver eyelids and cherry-red lips.

"I meant it." James and Edie walked up the stairs to the ballet. The San Francisco Ballet building was under construction, so they had moved to an old theater near Corona Heights Park. Perfect for their purposes. Shanice gave him careful instructions about what to do once inside.

"I don't sleep with anyone I work with." Edie turned on him. She stopped and sighed. "Sorry. Thank you. I can see you're genuine—I'm focused on the job right now." She brushed the shoulder of his tuxedo. It was one of the few items he had salvaged from his marriage. "You clean up nicely, too," she said.

Edie glanced at her phone before stashing it in her purse. "Let's go. Nia texted us to meet her by the bar at 9:10."

"There you are!" Edie and James spun round, bumping shoulders as they did so.

Girard. He also wore a tuxedo. James had tried to convince Edie, Esme, Nia, and Shanice he didn't need to dress up for the San Francisco Ballet. After all, it was the West Coast. Rich people walked around in yoga gear. But Shanice and Edie both insisted the tux would enhance his image. They said Girard would probably wear a tux since he was from the Northeast.

And, of course, they were right. Girard looked leaner and taller in the tux, perhaps because he stood next to a petite, round woman in a teal silk gown. Her lips were made up in a carmine bow, and her diamond ring was the size of a robin's egg. She leaned on Girard, nearly toppling over in her miniature stilettos as he leaned forward and shook their hands.

"Thanks again for the tickets," said Girard. "Myra was delighted our plans fell through so we could join you." James and Myra shook hands.

Girard turned to Edie. "And who is this vision?"

"Ah, this is my, ah, girlfriend." James choked out the words. He was out of practice—he hadn't used the word 'girlfriend' in twenty years.

"I'm Evie." Edie deftly preempted any further awkwardness from James. "Pleased to meet you. We appreciate you giving James this new job."

"He's doing me a favor." Girard winked at James. "Aren't you?"

"Let's go, dear." Myra had tired of the small talk. "I need to use the restroom before we find our seats."

Edie slipped her arm into Myra's, instantly melting away the stiffness Myra's body had taken on after her husband's leering introduction. "Me too. We'll go to- gether. We'll meet up with you boys later."

———

"How long have you known Fulton?" Edie silently pried open Myra's clutch and slid out the wallet from inside.

Fortunately for Edie, there was only one stall in the bathroom. And Myra was in it. It was also fortuitous that Myra had a clutch and nowhere to put it—except in Edie's hands.

"Fulton and I have been married for twenty-five years." Myra's voice was muffled through the thick oak door.

Edie let out a low whistle. "Impressive. Someday I hope to hit that number, too," she said, lying through her teeth as she snapped photos of Myra's driver's license and credit card with her phone.

"How long have you been dating James? He seems to be a nice young man. And handsome, too."

"Oh, ah, we've been together a year." A

tube of lipstick and an eyebrow pencil rolled onto the floor.

"Shit."

"What's wrong?"

"I dumped my bag on the floor."

Edie scrambled on the floor. She had the eyebrow pencil, but the lipstick had rolled under the sink behind the pedestal. If she could just . . .

Flush.

Edie's arm strained as she wrapped her hand around the base of the pedestal, fumbling for the tube.

The lock on the stall pulled back.

Edie had the lipstick now, hidden in her hand. She stood up just as Myra opened the stall door. The rest of the clutch was intact and closed. She handed the bag to Myra. Edie had a shoulder bag, so she waltzed into the stall and locked the door. Opening her hand revealed not only Myra's lipstick but a small piece of paper stuck to it. She jammed the tube and the paper into her own handbag.

"That's odd."

"What's odd?" Edie's heart raced.

"My lipstick's gone."

Silence.

"Oh well. I have another, and another in my bag. I find they're so much fun to buy. In fact, whenever I want candy, I buy myself a lipstick instead! I've lost five pounds that way," Myra prattled. "Though I gained another ten after I broke my ankle."

"Keeping weight off is hard." Edie focused on the time-honored distraction of weight-related talk.

"I'm sure you don't have any trouble with that, do you, dear?"

Edie opened the door. "I'm afraid the thin girl pose is all an act, Myra."

9

———————

James leaned back in his plush red seat and let out a whoosh of air.

"Comfortable, aren't they?" Girard pulled a bag from his pocket. "Care for some walnuts?" The cellophane made a loud crinkling noise.

"Ah, no, thanks, Fulton. We had a fantastic meal."

"Too bad. Walnuts are good for the digestion." He leaned over, closer to James. "Speaking of food. Your date is delicious. Where did you find her?"

James sniffed. "We've been dating for a year."

"Oh, sorry. I thought, you know . . . " He elbowed James with a 'we're-men-of-the-world' gesture.

"Darling, what fabulous seats," Myra squealed. James rose. "Here, please take my seat. I kept it warm for you." He gave her an awkward little bow.

James and Edie took their seats. The lights went down, and the orchestra struck up softly, steadily building to a crescendo.

Edie nudged James. She unfolded a slip of paper and turned on her phone. By the blue light of the phone, James read the words *James Bowman. Tisdale Partners.*

Edie mouthed, "It's from Myra."

James shrugged, feeling puzzled.

Edie shook her head, exasperated. She scribbled on a tiny notepad. James turned on his phone again so he could illuminate the note:

Why does she have your name on a slip of paper? Do you think she's checking up on you?

James shrugged. He scribbled back: *Maybe she was just trying to remember my name, so she wrote it down.*

Edie gave him a slow nod. Then she bent

down and slid out Myra's clutch from the space between the seats.

He watched Edie in horror.

Myra sneezed. Her hand slid over the arm of the seat toward the clutch.

"Here." Edie offered Myra a tissue packet.

How did she find a tissue so quickly?

"Thank you, dear."

Edie opened the edge of the clutch and popped the tube of lipstick and paper back into place.

James cocked his head to one side and raised his eyebrow. Edie held up her index finger.

Reaching into her own bag, she pulled out a pen and a blank business card. On one side she wrote her cell number. On the other side, she wrote: *Call me.*

Both of James' eyebrows rose this time. As the music swelled and ballerinas twirled in a mess of tulle on stage, Edie leaned over and slipped the card into Fulton's pocket.

She winked at James and whispered, "Let's take a bet. He'll call or text me within the next twenty-four hours."

"How much? Though I think I'll lose anyway."

"If I win, you make breakfast for me for a week. And I don't mean just any breakfast. Fancy."

"You're on."

She peered at her phone. "And so is Nia in ten minutes."

———

"Mmmmm . . . I could murder for a glass of champagne." Myra stumbled out of the darkness of the box seats and into the soft hallway lighting. People streamed into the hallway. Several lounged on benches, staring at their phones as if they had received the most important text messages of their lives.

Edie put a hand on Myra's shoulder and turned to James and Fulton. "We'll go to the bar for champagne and will save two glasses for you two."

James nudged Fulton. "I want to show you something special. Follow me."

Fulton's mouth twitched into a smile. "I'm always ready for something special. Lead on."

They wound their way downstairs

through an institutional beige stairwell with a stale, suffocating odor.

"Where are we going?" Fulton wiped his brow. James slowed down. Though Fulton was fit, he had to be at least sixty, perhaps older.

"Not much farther." James threw his weight against a heavy fire door. It creaked open. A great gush of fresh, cold air hit them as they moved onto a back terrace. Hedges lined the balcony with a few scattered tables covered in dust and bird droppings. They could see the bay, the Golden Gate Bridge, and the blinking lights of Angel Island in the distance.

Fulton sighed. "It's a beautiful view." He turned toward James and eyed him up and down. "But as beautiful as it is, is there a reason you brought me here?"

"See the building to the left of the large tower?"

"Yes—you mean that eyesore apartment building?"

"Yep. Do you know anything about it?"

"Nothing, except it's a monstrosity."

"It's for sale. It's low-income apartments. Juniper Downs."

"Well, poor people can't afford to live in this city anyway. We'd be doing them a favor by moving them out."

James gulped. "My feelings exactly. We'd be doing them a favor because eventually they won't be able to make ends meet at all, and then they'll be trapped."

"Glad to see we think alike." Fulton clapped him on the back and fumbled around in his pockets, eventually pulling out a silver cigarette case and lighter. He held a finger up to his lips. "Don't tell Myra. She'll kill me. Want one?"

James shook his head. "Your secret's safe with me, though we should go back to our seats."

Fulton was an expert quick smoker. Within seconds he had lit the cigarette and taken three practiced long puffs, almost like he was smoking a joint.

"Yes, we should go back. But these apartments are for sale. How much?"

"I'm not sure, but I know the broker. He has to handle publicity carefully these days. Want me to invite him to our little party? I already talked with Evie about planning it for this week. She's game."

Girard took a long drag on the cigarette before stamping it out with his gleaming leather shoe.

"I bet she is, James, I bet she is."

10

———

A side door opened in the dimly lit back hallway. Out marched, or rather waltzed, a coterie of ballerinas. They tiptoed like a stream of dutiful ducklings following their mother. White, pink, red, and black flashed before them. One ballerina dropped something. Something tiny clattered on the floor.

James ran over as it wheeled toward another open doorway. He scooped it up and held the gold ring aloft in triumph.

The ballerina slipped away from the duckling line toward James and Girard.

She wore a red tulle dress and red pointe slippers. Her hair was pulled back in expected ballet fashion. She had on such heavy eye makeup she resembled a baseball out-fielder on a summer's day. Exquisitely groomed eyebrows curved upward at the edges, emphasizing her cat-eye makeup.

"Thank you for finding my ring." She looked at James. "I must be on stage in a few minutes."

"No problem. This is Fulton," said James.

The ballerina surveyed him expectantly.

"Oh, and I'm James," he continued. "You were marvelous during the first part of the performance."

"My name is Belle. Let me buy you two a drink afterward as a thank-you for finding my ring."

Another ballerina bumped into Belle. They glared at each other.

"Yes, yes, we'd love that." Girard stared at Belle.

"Great. Meet back here after the performance. A bottle of whiskey awaits us in my dressing room."

Girard turned to James. "Lovely girl."

"We'd better find the other girls before they suspect we're making trouble."

———

JAMES AND GIRARD left their dates at the bar while they excused themselves again to discuss an urgent business matter. Girard looked as excited as a small child with a new toy. Belle popped out her head from around the corner and waved them down the hallway.

Nia's performance as Belle was flawless. She had converted a small broom closet into a dressing room by filling the walls with ballet paraphernalia. After offering the pair short stools, she pulled a flask from the side of what appeared to be a file cabinet.

Girard took the proffered glass. "I admit I didn't see you on stage during the second half of the performance."

"Oh, it's because I'm an understudy. She showed up right at intermission."

"How do you make ends meet as an understudy?" James nearly winked at Nia.

"It's not easy, that's for sure. My true passion is art."

"Isn't ballet art?" Girard smacked his lips after his first sip.

"Yes, of course. But I mean painting. I love painting murals—and creating public art exhibitions. Strictly what people call 'multicultural art' these days. But I call it art because it expresses my experience."

"Really?" Girard leaned forward. "Do you work for anyone right now?"

"There's this great new nonprofit. Or I guess you'd call it an art consulting firm. They're called SanCulture Consulting and Leadership. We call it SanCul. Have you heard of them?"

Girard shook his head. "I haven't been here long, so it's not surprising. Have you?" He glanced at James.

"SanCulture . . . Didn't they do something last year in the East Bay?"

"Yes, a series of big murals." Belle flung back the rest of her drink. "I've been contracting with them for a few months."

Fulton's eyes narrowed. "Belle. Could you give me your number?"

"Well . . ." She trailed off, shrinking into her tulle skirt.

Fulton's pale white face turned scarlet. "Ah, no. It's not what you think. I'd like to get your number in case something comes up— in the mural line of work, I mean."

Belle chuckled. "Oh, of course," she said, pulling out a pad of paper and pen from the filing cabinet. James wondered idly what else she might have in there.

She scribbled on the pad, tore off a sheet, and handed it to Girard as if she had given him a check for a million dollars.

"I'm sure we'll be in touch." Girard lifted his empty glass in salute to Belle.

"I'm sure we will be, Mr. Girard," she mumbled under her breath as she shut the door to the closet.

11

———————

Cigarette ash glowed in the inky black.

"Those things will kill you." James chuckled.

"Fuck you." Edie took a colossal drag on the cigarette.

"Sorry. I couldn't help it—I'm giddy after that."

"After what? And what do you mean by 'giddy'?"

"After putting on a show in there. I'm not used to it. And giddy means what happens when your blood rushes to your head."

"I'm not an idiot, James. I asked you to be more accurate in your description," she drawled as if she were a BBC announcer.

"Oh." He paused. "I seem to fuck up constantly, don't I?"

"Don't worry, you'll get used to it." She grinned and nudged him in the ribs. "You did pretty good in there. Though you could've ogled what's-her-face more. She was gagging for it. Positively giddy, as they say," she drawled again.

A figure lugging a mound of tulle rounded the corner of the ballet building. Nia's head peeked through the pile of skirts. "Can we get going? I know this looks light but believe me, it's heavy."

Edie stamped out her cigarette as James and Nia dumped the tulle in the trunk.

"Great parking spot, Edie," said Nia. "Must be the only illegal spot in San Francisco the ticket cops can't find. And a great view, too." City lights winked at them in the breathtaking view of the Presidio straight ahead and the Richmond District to the left.

"I call shotgun!" Nia rushed to the front seat.

Edie slid into the driver's seat while James folded his frame into the back seat. Nia adjusted the seat forward.

"Ah, thanks, Nia. You were amazing, *Belle*."

"Not too bad yourself, especially for your first time." She laughed and held up a stack of enormous oatmeal cookies. "See what I found! I didn't realize ballerinas ate cookies."

"I doubt it, since they left all of those," said Edie.

"Mmhhh . . ." Nia munched away on one and then another. "Want one?" She waved the stack at James.

"No, thanks. I feel like I'm on enough of a sugar high already."

Ca-thunk, Ca-thunk, Ca-thunk.

The rhythm of the car crossing the metal ties on the Golden Gate Bridge was always soothing. Soon they saw the rainbow tunnel ahead. James let out a heavy sigh.

Edie looked at him through the rearview mirror. "Relieved, aren't you?"

"Yes. I didn't realize how exhausting this job would be. I knew it would be hard, but not exhausting."

Nia waved her hand at James. "Follow my lead, and you'll be fine. Eat lots of cookies."

Edie rolled her eyes. "But seriously, tell

us why a respectable person like you got involved with a bunch of con artists like us?"

Nia leaned forward and bit into another cookie. "I'm dying to know. Shanice wouldn't tell me—she said you'd have to tell us the story."

"Alright. I'll tell you. On one condition."

"Name it," said Nia.

"That you tell the others so I don't have to relive the story again."

Nia and Edie nodded.

"I worked for Tisdale Partners in the city. I had a beautiful wife, Alana, and still do have a child, Katrina."

"How old is she?" asked Nia.

"She'll be six in about a month," he said and sighed. "So everything was wonderful, until one day I came home and found Alana in bed with another man. His name is Seth Hummel. He owns the rival company to the one I worked at. Called DesignNiche. I call it DesignShit, but that's neither here nor there."

"So sorry, James." Nia put a hand on his shoulder.

"If that had been it, I would have survived it somehow. I would have been willing to patch things up with Alana. But it was far from the end of the story. I went to a hotel that night to get my head straight. Around midnight I heard a knock at the door."

"It was Seth, wasn't it?" asked Edie.

"I wish it were Seth. No, it was the police. They had traced my credit card. Turns out Alana had put on makeup to look like she'd been beaten. In a previous life, she had worked as a makeup artist, so she knew how to make it appear real. She said I'd found out she'd been having an affair and that I'd beaten her. So the police hauled me off to jail. They released me when it was established this had been a one-time incident. My lawyer cast enough doubt on the beating by suggesting the bruises were makeup. I received six months' probation."

James saw Edie and Nia exchange worried glances in the mirror.

"If you two don't believe me, then it's better if you let me out of the car right now."

"It's just a reflex reaction, understand?" Edie gripped the wheel and turned hard as they drove off the freeway. "If Shanice trusts you, we trust you."

"Thanks." He mopped his brow with a

Kleenex. "So Alana not only got the house and everything else in the divorce that happened as soon as I received probation, but she also got custody of Katrina because I had received probation. I'm supposed to see her every once in a while, but that never happens."

"What happened to your job?" asked Nia.

"I was able to cover things up at the beginning. As soon as I could see things were going to get worse, I resigned so no one would find out anything. Besides, I knew if I stayed, Seth would pull some bullshit, not only because I worked at Tisdale but because it was a rival firm."

"So how did you meet Shanice?" asked Edie.

"As you can imagine, I'd hit rock bottom. I didn't have any money, and I was drinking. Even though I've never really been a drinker. One day, I was crossing the street in Oakland when I was hit by a bicycle. Shanice had seen the accident and immediately knew what to do. Then she rushed me to a nearby ER. I thought that was it. But when they discharged me, she was waiting there to take me home."

"That's Shanice all over," said Nia.

"On the way home, I poured out my story to her. I have no idea why I did it, but she was the only person who'd shown me any kindness in months. When I'd finished telling her, she asked me how badly I wanted revenge. I told her I wanted it more than anything else in the world."

"Aha! That's how she hooked you," said Edie.

"It worked. I told her I was ready for anything. She said she'd be in touch. About two weeks later, we met again. She said she had checked out my story—though how she did, I don't know."

Nia gripped James' seat. "Did she tell you famous grifter stories? Like the one about Tonia Sinclair?"

"Was she the one who conned her way into the high finance world and managed to get thousands of dollars transferred to people working at a grocery store?"

"Yep. She's my favorite."

"Yeah, she told me lots of those stories. She said she had a plan to put a crew back together. Sounded like she had worked with both of you at some point."

A wistful smile spread across Edie's face. "Yes, those were the good old days. Shanice and I ran a few jobs together. Just the two of us."

Nia choked on her cookie. "Just the two of you? I never knew that!"

"Ah, it's best we not talk about it. Those were good times, though I remember a few close calls."

James twisted around in his seat. "When did you work with Shanice?"

"I wouldn't say I worked with her, but let's say she helped me get out of a bad situation involving some shady loans in college. I followed her lead and she said if and when I was ready, we could work together. I called her a few months ago to just check in and she told me she was thinking of putting a crew together," said Nia.

"Why'd you say yes?" asked Edie.

"Personal reasons. Shanice saved my life and my bank account. And let's just say I want to learn from the best."

———

"I'VE NEVER BEEN SO happy to see the week-end." James sighed in between sips of coffee. The coffee was thick and strong. Just as he liked it.

He squinted as the morning sun hit his face.

"Don't get too comfortable." Nia ignored James' vampire-like reaction to the sunlight as she shoveled cereal into her mouth. "Shanice told us to meet in the living room. I think we'll actually discuss the plan."

Esme snuck up behind Nia and put a hand on her shoulder. "You should eat something more nutritious, honey." She shook her head.

"Don't worry, I have slices of bananas in here. See?" She held up her spoon with a white disc as proof.

Esme continued to shake her head, but smiled as she stirred cream into her coffee. She tapped the spoon and stuck it into the dishwasher. Then she leaned against the counter and surveyed the scene, holding the coffee cup to her lips.

"I bet they had disgusting coffee in the old folks home, didn't they, Miss Esme?" Nia sliced another banana into her cereal, causing drops of milk to splatter onto the counter. Esme averted her eyes.

"Oh yes, dear. It wasn't coffee. It didn't just look like dishwater. I suspect it really *was* dishwater. The meals . . ." she trailed off in a shudder.

Esme glanced down. James peered over the kitchen island. Opal sauntered in with an air of "the party may now begin." Edie followed behind her, though with less confidence about the morning.

"Morning," she mumbled, head down. She shook the silver coffeepot. "Hey! Where's the coffee?" She glared at James.

"Don't look at me! We're all drinking coffee. Here, I've finished mine, so I'll make more."

Edie stood with her eyes half open, unable to say much in return.

"Morning, everyone." Shanice strolled in, holding her usual mug. She wouldn't need any coffee—she was the tea drinker among them. "Let's sit in the living room. I've hooked up the TV to my laptop so we can get started."

As she walked out of the room, she peered over her shoulder. "Make sure you have your drug of choice already ingested—sugar, caffeine, whatever. And you should take notes."

Esme and Edie followed Shanice into the living room.

James leaned over the kitchen island and whispered to Nia, "Can you run through the basics one more time for me?"

Nia set down her spoon and stretched her neck from side to side. "Sure. So the mark is the one we're targeting for the con. The old saying 'you can't cheat an honest person' is the golden rule in picking a mark."

"Yep. Got it." He stuffed a handful of blueberries in his mouth.

"The roper is the one who usually identifies the mark. They're also the first one to contact the mark. Then there's the 'inside man'—inside person, despite how clunky it sounds."

"Am I the inside man?" James' voice rose in excitement.

"I doubt it." She patted his hand. "That's usually saved for the most experienced and the mastermind of the crew. That would obviously be Shanice. The inside person works 'the inside', but it really means the one who calls all the shots. They contact the mark about the plan details. Then there's the convincer, who seems unconnected to everyone else but encourages the mark. Sometimes, they're the so-called 'face', which means they're a honey trap. They're really helpful when the mark starts to doubt whether they should follow the plan."

"Haven't you forgotten the fixer?"

"Hey! Was saving the best for last. The fixer handles all the technical stuff, putting together leads and research. Probably the most important person, in my view."

"Why wouldn't they be the mastermind?"

"You could argue that, but we all know about the mastermind's plan—even if we don't have a clue about the details. We can help the mastermind see if there's a problem. The fixer, though, has a tougher job, because they do it on their own. And so many things can go wrong."

"Such as?"

"Someone changes a password, the internet goes down, or batteries die unexpectedly. Little things can have big consequences."

12

―――――

Once they settled into the L-shaped couches, Shanice cleared her throat. "Yes, it's that time." She let out a throaty laugh. "I realize I've snapped at you about the job, but it's because I have so much on my mind." Interesting, thought James. I wonder if she has trouble apologizing.

"With that sentimentality out of the way, let's begin." She aimed her clicker at the blank white wall and leaned back on one heel. James realized Shanice must have given hundreds of presentations in her previous life. Funny, he didn't think of doctors giving presentations all the time. But perhaps they did.

"James? Are you alright?" asked Shanice.

"Oh, yes. Sorry. Just thinking about last night."

The sun streamed through the bay windows, so Edie pulled down the blinds.

"Now, here's the situation." Shanice clicked to the first slide. "As we all know, the Bay Area is chock-full of marks, given the number of wealthy people and the cost of living. That means sharks have plenty of opportunities. Particularly our old friends: bankers, developers, and real estate agents. At first, I thought a developer would be our mark because they embody the idea of something for nothing." She gestured toward James with the clicker. "That's one reason we brought you on."

"But not the only reason." Nia waved her coffee mug.

"Thanks, Nia." James waved his coffee cup back at Nia.

Shanice didn't respond but pursed her lips. "James' developer connections means he's an ideal roper. Or roper intern, I should say."

"I'm the roper?"

Everyone laughed.

"Yes, James. You're a roper in training. Anyway, I couldn't figure out the developer angle. But through my research, I uncovered how the Planning Commission is a revolving door of developers and other high-finance people. Fulton Girard's name popped up. There are watchdogs on the commission, but genuine ones are hard to find."

"Fulton Girard? Who is he, some sort of knight?" Esme smiled. James wasn't sure if she was serious or joking.

Nia giggled. "I thought so too."

Shanice switched to a cheesy headshot of Girard. There was definitely something about that grin. His teeth were too big for his mouth so it forced back his lips into a canine smirk.

"Fulton Girard went to all the usual places: Harvard, then Yale for his MBA and a degree in city planning. There is a mysterious gap of about five years in his resumé. He was clearly involved in writing subprime mortgages, though. Before and after this five-year period, he joined local planning boards around New Jersey, particularly ones where there wasn't a whole lot of transparency. He'd present himself as a one-man lobbyist and expert to city officials seeking advice about how to 'revitalize' their local communities. Which usually meant pushing out poor people and people of color wherever they could."

Heads nodded around the room.

"The man is a positive genius in fixing the planning process so there are hundreds of developer loopholes. He builds his reputation as a policy guru so other planning commissioners seek him out for advice. He's so good he can tell a commissioner he's helping them with something—which he might be—but then insert a couple of lines or even a few strategically placed commas, which do something for himself or one of his cronies."

"Sounds like Congress." James sighed.

"Exactly. But that's the US Government, isn't it? One big gang against the others."

"But it's not so simple." James waved his mug around again, this time spraying droplets onto his pants.

Esme patted James on the shoulder. James decided it was wise to take this hint to be quiet.

"Doesn't James have a point?" Nia raised her hand.

Edie, Esme, and Shanice all shot her a look. Miss Esme cleared her throat. "You're still young, honey. You'll come to understand."

"I mean, I get the police are that way, but the whole country?"

Shanice made a slitting motion across her throat. "Let's save this discussion for late-night drinks, shall we? Though I don't know when we'll have time for that in the near future." She paused and gestured at the wall. "Back to our mark, Fulton Girard."

"But I thought you said we were interested in developers, not commissioners." James drummed his fingers on the arm of the couch.

"Yes, but the more I thought about it, the more I realized our purpose is to bring down a city official. After all, it's easy to point at the evil gentrifying developers—and I'm not letting them off the hook—but city officials allow this to happen. Girard's specialty is to tear down low-income housing to 'revitalize' it."

"Last night, Girard said it would be a favor to low-income people to tear down Juniper Downs. Because they'd be priced out eventually anyway and have nowhere to go."

"Well, that's exactly the kind of bullshit he spews."

"What do we get out of the con? And how does it help the people who live in Juniper Downs?" asked Nia.

"Excellent question." Shanice rubbed her forehead. James noticed faint lines on her forehead for the first time.

"My auntie lives in Juniper Downs," said Shanice. "An eighty-year-old fighter. I bet she'll make it to a hundred."

Esme lifted her orange juice glass. "I'll drink to that!"

Shanice gave her a wan smile. "But my auntie told me they're constantly being threatened with eviction, every time a developer starts to sniff around. She's afraid it's only a matter of time before they win. Especially now that Mayor Santos is no longer mayor."

"Can they organize to keep out the developers?" asked Edie.

Shanice shook her head. "They've had some success—when Santos was in office—but I'd say seventy-five percent of the residents are sixty-five and over. It's hard because they aren't really that mobile and don't have a lot of energy."

"I'm all in," said Nia, "but what do we get out of it?"

"We save my auntie's home—and not just temporarily—and we get some cash to boot."

James wondered about revenge against Alana that he had been promised. But he was too sheepish to ask.

"What's his weakness?" Esme raised her hand.

"Whose weakness?" asked Edie.

"Ah, Miss Esme always gets to the point. Girard's weakness is . . ." She clicked to the next slide, clearly relishing this moment.

"Women." Edie's eyes were still at half-mast. "By the way, James, I won the bet. He texted me this morning."

"Already? That was quick."

Shanice smiled. "Yes, women are his first weakness, which, frankly, isn't all that interesting in a mark. Too predictable. Not women per se, but a weakness for cheating."

Esme groaned. "A honey trap?"

"No, no." Shanice waved her clicker dismissively. "That might need to be part of it, but his other intriguing weakness is art collecting. Makes him greedy. Or it could be the other way around—maybe he's greedy so he collects art."

"What kind of art?" asked Edie.

"He owns an original Basquiat, two Warhols, and two of Kusama's pumpkins."

"How'd you find that out?" James leaned forward.

Shanice looked at Esme. She shrugged. "I know my way around Google. And with Edie's photos of Myra Girard's ID, it was a snap."

A knock came at the door.

13

The knocking became banging.

Everyone's heads swiveled around and their bodies stiffened.

James rose and padded to the door. They had selected this house because the entryway was set off from the rest of the building. Shanice also appreciated multiple exit points. They had hoped their ability to rent a large home in Mill Valley would keep prying eyes away.

"Who is it?" James used his most casual voice. The knock hadn't made him nervous, but everyone else's reactions made him jumpy.

"Police."

Shit.

He could hear his own breath. Silence enveloped the house.

Something tickled his feet. Opal.

Without thinking, he scooped up Opal and put her on his shoulder. He winced at her claws, but thought it would make him look friendly.

Clunk. He slid back the deadbolt and opened the door slowly.

A stout officer in a uniform stood closest to him. She wore a long blond braid, giving her a formidable Norse Goddess appearance. Brunhilda. James wondered if she had sucked on a lemon for breakfast. Next to her stood an equally stout man with a pasty white face, who could use the hipster-hip-pie-health-craze advice dispensed in Marin County.

"Yes, officers? How may I help you?" Opal crawled along the back of James' neck from one shoulder to another as if she were a trained monkey.

"We had a report of a disturbance, sir." Brunhilda didn't glance up from her clipboard.

"At nine on a Saturday morning? What kind of disturbance?"

"Noise."

James' jaw dropped. "Really, Officer? We haven't been playing music. In fact, the one person who likes loud music always wears headphones since we enjoy quiet. Besides, Mill Valley code, section F, titled *Noise Arising From Residential Activities* specifies that certain types of activities and noise sources associated with residential living, although not considered acceptable by most residential inhabitants, are, nevertheless, tolerated." He paused. "And I can't imagine any sound from our house exceeds Table A-2 limits."

The unhealthy officer ignored James' lengthy recitation. "How many residents in the house, sir?"

"There's—" James stopped. "Why should I tell you? Shall I cite the code about the number of people allowed to visit a mansion?"

"This isn't a mansion, sir." Brunhilda flipped her braid behind her back.

"It costs more than a mansion."

"Are you renting, sir?" The pasty officer doodled flowers on his clipboard.

Edie popped her head over James' shoulder. "What seems to be the trouble, officers? Has James been a bad boy?" She positively cooed.

Brunhilda stared at Edie hungrily, while Pasty Face continued to scribble.

"Excuse me, where are my manners? This is my wife, Eden Talcott. And I'm James Ambrose." He hoped the introductions would reset the conversation.

"Pleased to meet you, officers." Edie offered a hand to each officer.

Neither officer responded.

"Officers Schmidt and Hasties." Brunhilda fumbled with the radio on her chest.

Some garbled nonsense played over the radio at top volume. James thought the officers themselves should be given a citation for noise disturbance.

Brunhilda put her lips against the radio. "No. Yes." She lifted her chin at Officer Hastie, signaling it was time to go.

"Ah, Mr. Bowman, Ms. Talcott, please be aware of your noise level. And remember the restrictions on the number of residents. We shouldn't have to come out here again—the first time is a friendly warning." Schmidt turned on her heel and marched toward the patrol car. Hastie padded behind her, waving his clipboard as he went.

James nodded at Edie as he closed the door. "Thanks."

"No problem. Just remember not to engage them in conversation. Or argue. They'll trap you in your own web of lies."

He nodded and wiped his brow.

"All clear? Did one of our white neighbors call to complain about us? Or was it just straight-up police harassment?" asked Shanice.

"Could have been either. Hard to tell." Edie plopped onto the couch without further explanation.

Shanice grimaced and shrugged. "Let's get back to planning."

Nia slapped her hands on her thighs. "Yes! I'm ready for our party planning."

"In a minute. We'll combine Girard's love of art and his love of money into one big con."

"We'll sell him a fake painting?" Esme rubbed her hands together.

"Not quite. We'll sell him mural art."

Shanice clicked to the next slide. The word *artwashing* flashed across the screen.

"Never heard of it." Edie put a finger to her lips.

Everyone else shook their heads.

Shanice clicked through to various developments around the world with buildings covered in bright murals. "Street art is used to placate developers, the media, and new residents when a developer wants to tear down low-income housing in the middle of the city, for example. They hire local artists to create art installations at the site, building excitement and making the whole process seem natural." She flipped through more cityscapes.

"So we'll be artwashers, too?" Nia had twisted her leg behind her neck.

"Mmmhhh." Shanice nodded. "But we need a front organization. We set up Nia to meet Girard at the ballet so we'd have a lead in our new organization." She flipped to the next slide, *SanCulture Consulting & Leadership*. "We call it SanCul for short. I'll be the director. Edie is a board member, and Nia is the artist."

"What about Miss Esme? And me?" James squeaked.

"Miss Esme is our fixer. She's also playing the outside role. You've already in deep, James."

"Won't we need planning permission for the art installation?" James shifted uncomfortably in his seat. "I haven't a clue about how to obtain permission. And it'll draw attention to us."

Esme patted James on his thigh. "Don't worry, sweetie, Shanice's got it all worked out just fine."

14

The Girards' Victorian mansion loomed over the black Mercedes as the crew circled the block for the thirtieth time. Fingers of fog crept along the roof and around the small turret. The fog blocked the view of the top, but the rest of the Sea Cliff mansion's bases were visible.

James shifted the gears of the car into park. "We'll never find a space at this rate. Where did you get a Mercedes, anyway?"

"Zippercar," said Shanice without flinching a muscle on her face.

"Very funny." James glanced behind him. "I shouldn't have asked. But seriously, where can we park? Why don't you all get out and I'll circle until I find something."

"Are you crazy?" Miss Esme leaned forward from the back seat. "You're our ticket in." She paused, surveying Edie. "Well, other than Edie here, who certainly has an invitation into Girard's bed."

Edie snorted. "Not if Mrs. Girard can help it. Why don't I park and you all go in? It will build the suspense for Mr. Girard."

"He'll get upset I left you to find a space."

"We'll let him. He'll think you mistreat me. Or you can say I have magical parking powers."

"Let's do it already. I want to get this party started—and done with as soon as possible." Shanice wiggled out of the car in black jeans, heels, red floaty caftan top, and long necklace. This had been Nia's handiwork—Shanice said she didn't know how to dress the part. As she walked in front of the car, she wobbled on the three-inch heels. Looking up at the stairs to the mansion, she shook her head and returned to the car.

"Nia—hand me those low wedges. I haven't worn heels in years and I'm not about to wobble and fall over Fulton Girard. Or make a spectacle of myself."

Nia reached underneath her seat and offered Shanice the gray wedges. "Ahhh, much better." Shanice pointed the three-inch offending heel at James. "Lesson number one hundred and sixty-seven for you. Be comfortable in your own skin or people will see right through you."

Affirmations floated from the back seat.

The crew got out of the car. Edie screeched away in the Mercedes.

"That girl has issues," hissed Esme under her breath.

"Don't we all, Miss Esme. C'mon. It's time for us to all meet our mark together." Shanice tugged her earring and stared at each pair of eyes looking at her in wonder. "Ready?"

They nodded. Arm in arm, Esme and Shanice took the lead. James inhaled the damp air and smiled at Nia. They marched up the stone stairs to the sounds of jazz floating from the windows.

———

"JAMES, DARLING!" Myra tippled toward him on impossibly high heels. She wore an iridescent blue wrap with a high collar, making her look like queen of the mermaids. James' ex, Alana, had taught him a lot about clothing, and he secretly enjoyed it—though he didn't want to admit it.

The pile of coats and bags in the corner indicated the party had already started. People were filing in and out so Shanice, Nia, and Esme stood behind him in a single-file greeting line.

Myra gave him air kisses. Her champagne dripped onto his shoes. "So glad you made it. And who are these lovely people?" Her plasticine smile was so frozen she had probably been wearing it for three hours already—and likely couldn't change if she had wanted to.

"This is Jasmine Jacobs and this is her mother, Ms. June Frazier." James moved aside so the two of them could move forward. "Jasmine is the director of the arts consulting firm I was telling your husband about."

"Pleased to meet you both." Myra shook

their hands. "What's the name of the consulting firm, Jasmine?"

"SanCulture Consulting and Leadership. We started in LA, but we just opened up a branch in San Francisco."

"Hmm . . . I have plenty of contacts in LA, but I haven't heard of it."

James held his breath.

Myra shrugged. "Oh well, I'm sure we'll find out more. Besides, Fulton is the real art expert." She waved her hand around the room erratically. Paintings covered the walls with little space in between them. "And who is this? You look familiar."

"I was at the ballet the other night— maybe you saw me there. I'm Belle Williams. I'm an understudy at the ballet, but—"

"She's our artist during the day." Shanice gave Nia a side hug.

"Yes, I work with Jasmine. I'd be thrilled to see the art collection."

"Well, Fulton might lead a tour later if you're lucky." Myra waved them all inside. "Now, go through the living room to the back. That's where the drinkies live. Make yourselves at home." After toasting them with a glass of prosecco, she continued the

"Darlings!" and air kisses with each new guest who traipsed through the door.

They weaved through the crowd, who were already bathed in the warm glow of alcohol. James noticed people glancing at them curiously, while doing their very best "I'm not looking at you" San Francisco stare. Charlie Parker played in the background and the crowd, while more dressed up than your average West Coaster, were still the types who spent a thousand dollars on a dowdy pair of shoes.

The paintings, framed and unframed, were a rich red hue, giving the expansive living room a warm, homey effect. He snatched a spring roll from one of the passing trays and popped the whole thing in his mouth.

"James. Are you ready?"

"Mmph."

The assortment of beverages was overwhelming. James imagined what Girard might drink so he could mimic him, but he was stumped. The man was clearly an old-school scotch drinker—not a hipster distillery scotch drinker, either—but he also had a smoothie on his desk. But James remembered Girard was a secret smoker, so opted for the scotch. Besides, he wasn't driving.

Nia chose a spritzer, Shanice a glass of white wine, and Esme a bourbon. They all clinked glasses.

Someone tapped James' shoulder.

"So glad you could come! I see you've brought some people with you—and I hope there's more." Girard leaned over and whispered in his ear, "Where's your lovely date?"

"Oh, she's parking the car."

Fulton's eyebrows lifted at least two inches. "Hope she finds a space soon. Now. Where are those developers and consultants you wanted me to meet?" James sipped his drink.

Crash.

Glass tinkled on the floor as the bourbon snifter slipped from Esme's fingers. Esme herself now lay on the floor, eyes closed and arms akimbo.

Nia, Shanice, and one of the caterers rushed over. Shanice felt the back of Esme's forehead and then leaned closer to her face.

"She'll be alright—she faints occasionally. I shouldn't have let her have any alcohol." Shanice craned her neck. "Is there somewhere upstairs we can carry her? I know she'll be fine—no need to call an ambulance."

Girard stepped forward. "Yes, of course. Are you sure we shouldn't call someone?"

Shanice shook her head.

"Then follow me." Girard declined to help Esme as Nia, the caterer, and Shanice struggled to lift her up. James held Esme's shoulder. It was the first time he saw Girard act in the way he expected a mark to act. Selfishly. And not just in words but in action.

They lumbered through the back hallway and up the spiral staircase. Esme must have weighed no more than a hundred pounds but it was still awkward to maneuver her round and round the staircase. When they reached the top, Girard had already disappeared down the hallway. Shanice scowled at James. James shrugged. Girard's selfishness was why they selected him as a mark, wasn't it?

Girard popped his head out of a doorway down the long hall and waved them toward him. A small guest room with a four-poster bed awaited Esme. James saw her eyes flicker.

They placed her on the bed gently and Nia removed her shoes.

"I'll stay with her." Shanice wiped Esme's brow with concern and turned to the caterer with a smile. "Thanks for your help."

The four of them filed into the hallway. The caterer stood there for a moment but took the hint at Girard's dismissive glance. Girard clasped Nia's hands. "Belle. So good of you to come. Let's go back downstairs and rejoin the party, shall we?"

15

Shanice tiptoed to the door and poked her head out.

"All clear."

Esme leapt out of bed. She snapped a few photos of paintings around the room. A Derrick Adams here and a Takashi Murakami there. And a beautiful figurine of a pumpkin on the mahogany desk.

"Let's check the other rooms at the end of the hall," whispered Shanice. She held up one finger. Voices floated up the stairs. Closer. Shanice winced at the "click" noise from the door as she shut it.

"There's an exquisite statue I want to

show you in the bedroom," said a high-pitched voice.

"I'll show you something exquisite in the bedroom," said an equally high-pitched voice.

Giggles.

Shanice rolled her eyes at Esme. "They're not going to . . . ? Are they?"

Esme shrugged. "Let's try the other end." A door clicked shut at the end of the hallway.

Shanice and Esme tiptoed past the bathroom to the first room. Shanice pushed the door—already open a crack—with one finger. It swung open slowly, revealing a study. A massive oak desk filled the center of the room. Bookshelves lined one wall and paintings the other. Shanice sniffed. A light cigarette smoke smell.

Esme made a beeline for the laptop as Shanice snapped more photos of the paintings.

"It's his personal computer!" Esme slid into the seat and tapped away happily on the keyboard.

Shanice smiled. "I'll find the master bedroom. I want to get a feel for his character.

Remember the drill if someone finds you here?"

Esme nodded at Shanice as an adult does when they're engrossed in a task—and not really listening to their child. She continued to tap away at the keyboard, using two fingers. Though Esme was an accomplished computer hacker, she still found two fingers more efficient than learning the 'new' way.

Blessing the plush carpets beneath her feet, Shanice finally found the master bedroom at the opposite end of the hallway. As expected, an enormous four-poster bed dominated. Oddly enough, only a few paintings adorned the walls in here, save a round oil painting of a child at the beach.

She peeked into the bathroom and was met by a wall of ammonia. White porcelain and silver chrome gleamed. She opened the cabinets gingerly to find anti-anxiety pills prescribed to Myra, a raft of vitamins, creams, and various makeup products.

The walk-in closet revealed a spare, but tasteful, assortment of Girard's clothes, while Myra's side was jam-packed with every type of fashion imaginable. And acres of heels.

Only the nightstands remained. One side

held an ereader, glass of water, sleeping pills, and a *Meditation Bedtime Ritual* book. The drawers were mostly empty. She twisted the knob on the other nightstand door.

A vast array of colorful plastic objects tumbled out. Sex toys. And not just a few. The cabinet on the nightstand held at least fifty.

Murmured voices came from the hallway. Shanice froze.

They were coming toward her.

Swallowing her nausea, Shanice stuffed the toys into the cabinet.

"And next, we have the master bedroom." Sounded like Girard.

Her head twisted around, seeking a place to hide. She must hide under the bed. She took a deep breath and slid in on her belly. It was awkward, to be sure, but she finally wedged herself underneath. Shanice now understood the purpose of those weird skirts around the bottom of a bed.

The door opened. "And here we are," Girard said.

"It's lovely. And it has a fantastic view of the bay."

Shanice stopped some involuntary exclamation from burbling up. It was Edie.

"Mmmh, you can say that again."

Her heart stopped. A small green vibrator had escaped her cleanup. The vibrator sat a foot away from her.

Not only did her heart stop, but so did her breathing. Girard—or Edie—though she guessed it was Girard, had sat on the bed.

"The view is even better from over here," said Girard.

"I bet it is," said Edie with an innocent, breezy air. Shanice saw high heels walk toward her and then stop at the vibrator. The heels kicked the vibrator under the bed, hitting Shanice squarely in the nose. She was sure she would either cry out or sneeze.

"There aren't many paintings in here. Let's see the other rooms."

"You're such a tease, Evie."

16

"Fulton! There you are. Let me introduce you to my former boss at Tisdale Partners. Fulton Girard, Abner Maxey. Abner Maxey, Fulton Girard." The two men shook hands.

Abner Maxey stood at least a foot shorter than the tall and wiry Girard. His stocky build, jowls, and round head made him a dead ringer for Winston Churchill. Hell, the man even smoked cigars. James found it odd cigars were still considered an indulgence, a luxury, while cigarettes were simply the devil. Wealth made a big difference.

"Pleased to meet you, Maxey. James has told me you're a developer to watch." Girard eyed Maxey's cigar hungrily.

"By watch, I hope you mean in the positive sense of the word." Abner tapped the cigar on an ashtray. James hadn't seen an ashtray in years.

"Oh yes, of course. Sometimes I forget I'm on the Planning Commission myself. I've been a developer all my life. Or, at least, involved in real estate in some way." Girard shrugged as if everyone naturally became a real estate agent when they grew up.

"So why'd you join the commission? Major cut in pay, and that's hard to afford in the Bay Area."

"Good old public spirit?" Girard asked the question of himself. "A developer brings a unique perspective to the Planning Commission. When I saw the city commission was filled with nonprofit types, I stepped up."

"Mmmm . . . and good for the city, too, in my opinion." Abner snatched a bruschetta from a passing tray. "And you're from Jersey, aren't you? What would make you come out here? East Coast is so different—life is too fast there."

"I love the East Coast, but Myra's family

is from out here. I told her I'd try it for a while. Feels like a more healthy lifestyle."

"Hmph. Health nuts everywhere. A bunch of bullshit, if you ask me."

James surveyed Abner—his physique reflected this sentiment. A man to live by his principles, he laughed to himself.

"So I told Fulton about your project. The land is worth at least fifty million. And it'll only increase, right?"

"Damn right." Abner's jowls jiggled. "But it's the fucking publicity and red tape we have a problem with."

"That's where the commission comes in handy." Girard then backtracked. "Not that I mean we can get around the rules, but I can help, well, shall we say, speed up the process?"

Abner nodded with a knowing smile.

"And we've had a brainwave about the publicity angle," said James, hoping this would prompt Girard. And it did.

"Excuse me." Girard rose. "I need to find that woman—Jasmine. Be back in a minute." Girard ambled toward the kitchen. The glassed-in back porch had a glorious view, and heaters sat between the tables. James motioned to the closest table. Especially since it had an empty ashtray.

Abner leaned over so close James thought his cigar would lodge in his ear. "Girard seems like a good one. Can he be trusted? I've had a look into his background, but you've probably already got a good feeling for him."

James mulled over what to say next, giving himself extra time by draining his glass of scotch. "Depends on what you mean by trust. I mean, when it comes down to it, who can really be trusted for anything?"

"True. But government work has already made you go all philosophical. What I mean is plain and simple. You know I'm a plain and simple man. When the chips are down, will he back us or will he cave to public pressure if things go south?"

Weaving his way through these mixed metaphors, James said cautiously, "You heard him say it himself. He sees himself as different than all the other commissioners." He pointed to a white woman in a flowing purple concoction with red hair and terrier-like movements in the corner. "I mean, compare Girard to Maggie Lambert over there.

She sees herself as the people's candidate, though I doubt she knows what that really means."

Abner nodded and licked his lips. James was encouraged, so he went on. "And what about James Chu over there? He's a small businessman, but is a stickler for the rules. Doesn't understand the big picture. And Theresa Quejada over there. Not a chance. She sees herself as diametrically opposed to developers, even though she's at this party."

"So you're saying he's already built himself a reputation as a developer's voice on the commission." Abner smoothed out the tablecloth in a rhythmic motion. He stopped suddenly as Girard returned. This time with Shanice.

"Abner Maxey, Jasmine Jacobs. Ms. Jacobs is director of SanCulture Consulting and Leadership. An arts consulting firm."

"Pleased to meet you, Ms. Jacobs." Abner shook her hand but gave James a perplexed look.

"Jasmine's fine, thank you." Shanice crossed her legs and settled back into a chair.

"I've been telling Jasmine about the opportunities to partner on new building projects around the city. Art beautifies ugliness, doesn't it, Jasmine?" Girard eyed a passing woman in a tight skirt.

James detected the slightest twitch in Shanice's eyelid. "Definitely. And I can tell by your painting collection, Mr. Girard—sorry, Fulton—you really mean it. And we can help. We've had several successful art launches in LA. I can tell you about them later, if you like."

In a flurry of purple, James saw someone bump into Abner's head.

"Oh, I'm so sorry." Maggie Lambert leaned over, nearly covering Abner's body in purple chiffon. "I've spilt my drink all over your beautiful suit." She tried to wipe it with her fingers as she bobbed and weaved. The woman was trashed. Girard, beet-red, handed Abner a stack of napkins.

As Abner dabbed at his suit, Maggie waved her champagne flute about. "I'm so sorry, Mr.—ah—"

"Maxey. Abner Maxey." He didn't look up from his shoulder.

"My God! *You're* Abner Maxey? I'm Maggie Lambert. I'm on the Planning Commission."

"Yes, I know you." He tilted his head upward only slightly. "I've learned a lot about planning commissioners. I make it my business."

A flash of sobriety passed across Maggie's face. "So you must know, then, I'm not a fan of yours." Her words were becoming more slurred. "And what you did to the Richmond District is a crime, sir. A crime of the highest order!" She had worked herself into a froth of fluttering chiffon, and the wrath of a mean drunk. James glanced at Shanice. They jumped up and nearly grabbed her by each arm.

"Oh dear, you won't believe what he's done to Black people, dear." She put her face so close to Shanice's that James feared Maggie might bite off her nose.

That was enough to prompt action. Shanice grabbed Maggie's arm. "Why don't you tell me all about it in the living room, *dear*," she said, voice dripping with sarcasm. Shanice gave James a slight head-nod that indicated he should stay.

He let go and sank back into his chair. Despite his embarrassment, Maggie had impeccable timing.

"What a bitch." Girard spit out the words. James felt cheered by his exclamation. His estimation of the man's moral character was falling like an elevator with a broken cable.

"You can say that again." And then for good measure, Abner repeated it.

"This is exactly why I'm so glad I came to meet you at this party. We have to deal with nutcases like Maggie Lambert. They constantly stall progress." Abner paused. "And they certainly can't hold their liquor."

17

Esme sucked in air and pursed her lips.

She pushed one finger on the keyboard, furiously, then another. The man hadn't password-protected any document. It was a goldmine, so she uploaded everything to a USB stick. While waiting, she rummaged around in the desk drawers. Not much there. There wouldn't be, these days—people didn't leave old receipts or notes hanging around much since everything was digital. She sighed.

Two more minutes to go.

Absently, she browsed Fulton's web history over the past week. Bingo.

•   •   •

SanCulture Consulting – 5 visits
  Belle Williams search – 2 visits
  James Bowman – 2 visits
  Arts murals and developers – Google search

ESME CHUCKLED out loud at the last entry of interest:

EVIE LENNOX – 10 visits

AS NOTHING more sparked her interest, she swiveled in the captain's chair and surveyed the room. Esme had never been an art fan, but she admired the arrangement of paintings in the office. She rose and perused the first oil painting collage—a colorful abstract lighting up the room.

Creak.

Someone was coming up the stairs. Esme ran back to the desk—the upload was nearly complete.

Footsteps approached.

She scanned the room but the only

hiding place was the enormous desk. She grabbed the computer, leaving it open so it would still download, and dove underneath the desk.

Heavy breathing. Almost wheezing.

The footsteps approached the desk. Esme tightened into a little ball. She snapped the computer shut because it wouldn't fit under the desk. One step closer. The breathing stopped. She heard a scratching noise and the wheezing resumed. A zipping sound came from near the doorway, and then the footsteps and breathing faded.

Esme stayed in a fetal position, wincing at her stiff joints. She slowly unbent and poked her head up over the mahogany desk.

She was just lifting herself onto the chair when the door opened.

———

"Esme!"

Shanice pulled Esme to her feet.

"What were you doing under the desk? Did someone find you?"

Esme nodded, catching her breath.

"Someone came in, but I uploaded everything in time."

"Who came in?"

"I don't know, but they must be large judging by their footsteps and breathing."

"Did they search for the computer?"

Esme adjusted her glasses. "They came close to the desk, but didn't open any drawers."

Shanice gazed around the room. She pointed at a nail on the wall. "I think they found what they wanted. Do you remember which painting hung in that spot?"

Esme shook her head.

Shanice crossed her arms and stared at the empty space on the wall.

"I forgot you have a photographic memory."

"Trying hard." Shanice squinted at the nail. "I wasn't in the room for long." She rubbed her forehead. "If you look at its placement on the wall." She touched the nail. "You can see it was probably a tiny painting."

"Logical since it would be hard to smuggle a large painting."

Esme grabbed Shanice's arm. "You don't think it was Edie, do you?"

18

Nia wrinkled her nose. The bar held a heady mixture of beer and sweet cocktails in a room that hadn't experienced ventilation in forty years.

"Ow." He bumped his head on the low-slung ceiling. He still piloted the drinks without losing too much liquid.

"What *is* this place?" Nia scooted into the booth-like bench in the corner. Esme followed suit on one side, and Edie and Shanice on the other.

"It's the Clover." Shanice saluted. "An institution. A survivor. This bar opened in the 1940s, and has somehow avoided being shut down by the police or developers. It's so hard to see from the outside that I think most people ignore it."

"C'mon, Shanice." Edie sipped a pint of urine-colored beer. "There must be more to it. I know you. Bars like this don't survive eighty years without help."

The left corner of Shanice's mouth lifted. "OK, you win. Every bar like this needs a little protection, doesn't it? Let's just say they have connections."

"It's a grifter's bar," said Esme in a hushed but matter-of-fact tone. "Every time someone tries to buy it or threatens to shut it down, the clientele make sure the bar stays open."

James surveyed the scene. Dive bar was the word. And truly a dive, not some former dive taken over by hipsters and reclaimed as the 'original' dive bar which then drives away the people who first made it a dive. A film of dust, grime, and alcohol lay over the tables, chairs, and benches. The floor had a slightly sticky quality that comes from never having a deep clean. Especially after almost eighty years. The old-timer at the bar who nursed a glass of port—an eccentric choice in a place like this—looked like he had been sitting on the stool since 1940.

The bartender was considerably younger but had the wary, watchful eye of someone much older. He had a towel positioned over his shoulder like he would be ready to snap it at any of the customers should they get out of hand.

In the opposite corner sat two men in their fifties, one bald and one with a cap pulled down over his eyes. They gesticulated wildly, but talked in a whisper.

"So we're safe to talk here is what you're saying." Edie brought James back into the conversation.

"Mmmhhh. Tell me if you noticed anything strange at the party. Because we have to really put the plan into action tomorrow, and I don't want to unless we're sure we can keep going."

Esme sipped an orange juice. "I'll have a look at everything I downloaded tomorrow, but I saw by Fulton's browsing history he's been checking out the right websites. He has hit on our fake websites, and has also been researching your fake background pages." She pointed at James and Edie.

"So the honey trap has been working." Nia cracked a peanut shell and popped its contents into her mouth.

"A little too well for my taste." Edie took a large gulp of her beer.

"Tell me about it." Shanice broke into a grin. "I was afraid you two might get a little too close on the bed when I was stuck underneath it."

Edie rolled her eyes. "Ugh. I'm so glad he didn't try anything. But I can only string him along for so long, so I'm glad we're moving quickly to really get rolling tomorrow."

James twisted his beer glass around in a rhythmic motion. "What's with the other commissioners? Do they come into this at all? I mean, the drunken scene with Maggie. . ."

"They're really just props, but willing props, as far as I can see. And they helped make our case—that Girard should trust Maxey and vice versa."

"It was excellent timing," said James, absently.

"What is it? Why are you staring into your glass?" Shanice lowered her chin and peered into James' eyes.

"Hmmm?" He glanced up. "Oh, I don't know. I'm new at this game of course, but . . ."

"Look." Nia suddenly sat up straight. "This will work only if we're honest. Begin to trust your instincts. Isn't that right, Miss Esme?"

Esme nodded.

James twisted his glass on the sticky table. "Well, I found it too coincidental. How come drunken Maggie came up to us just at the right moment?"

Shanice smiled at James.

"What? Why are you staring at me?"

"Because I wondered if you would pick up on it." Shanice lifted her glass and everyone clinked. "It was strange, but I'm not sure what it means yet."

"You can be maddening sometimes, right, Shanice?" James took his obligatory sip.

Esme chuckled. "Ah, the impatient intern. A good role for you, Mr. Bowman." Then she leaned her frame back against the wooden bench. "My question is different. What does the missing painting mean?"

Edie lowered her voice. "It means we're not the only ones who weren't what they seemed at the party."

19

———————

"Why aren't we at the Port of San Francisco?" Nia kicked a rock on the sidewalk.

James wondered why as well. They stood on Middle Road, a bleak, industrial stretch running alongside the Port of Oakland. The fence wasn't exactly secure. It looked like the city had invested money one year in fixing the fence but had only gotten so far before the budget was yanked.

Shanice pulled down her baseball cap over her eyes and squinted at Nia in the bright morning sun. "Oakland is huge compared to San Francisco. And easier to access." She rattled the bent chain-link fence. Then she adjusted her blue uniform, a gas station uniform badge embroidered with *Sally* on her shirt. Nia's read *Jamie*, and James' read *Roberto*.

"C'mon, Bob." Shanice gave James a light bump on the arm. "Time for you to prove yourself."

"Again?" whined James.

Nia and Shanice just laughed. Crossing their arms, they waved James in toward the fence.

"There aren't any security cameras here, so you'll be fine. Keep your cap down over your eyes."

"If you told me why I need to steal the ID badges, it would be a lot easier," said James.

Shanice pursed her lips. "Alright. I might as well tell you. We need a shipping container for the artwashing project. If we try to buy one, it can be traced. So we need the badges so we can legitimately pick up a container and drive off with it. We'll handle the pickup. All you have to do is find the badges." Shanice looked up and down the street. "You'd better get going. Some-one's walking toward us. They don't work for the port, though, so no need to worry."

He grimaced as he slid through the

fence. Crouching down, he put one foot in front of another. Except one foot wouldn't move. Dammit, it was caught on the fence.

Nia leaned over to unhook his pant leg.

"Hurry!" hissed Shanice. "They're coming. And they have a dog."

"Shit, shit, shit." Nia desperately twisted the wire on the cut piece of fence. James jerked his leg.

"Don't do that! It makes it worse." Nia's hole in the fence was wider now.

James heard a low growl.

"What a beautiful dog," Shanice said. "Is it alright if I pet her?"

The response sounded somewhere in between a grunt and a snort.

"Whaddeya all doing anyway?" a slurred voice asked.

"Oh, my friend fell over onto the fence. He's always tripping over everything."

The dog growled again. This time with more menace.

"He doesn't like your hat." The slurred voice turned belligerent. "You'd better take it off."

"It's OK." Shanice's voice rose an octave.

"I'd better help my friend up, since she's not having much luck."

The scraping of a dog's toenails on the pavement ebbed away. James breathed a sigh of relief. But he was still stuck.

"Here." Shanice leaned over his leg. She whipped out a Swiss army knife, opened one blade and sawed away at his pant leg.

"Hey! Those are my pants!"

"Would you rather have your pants or be caught for trespassing?"

James couldn't respond. Soon he was free. He crouched down near the fence, sneezing from the dust billowing around him. Among the stacks of colorful containers, a clear pathway wound its way forward. Shanice said he needed to follow the pathway, take a left and then a right and he would arrive at a small office. At least according to Google Earth.

He soon arrived at a tollbooth-like office. From the corrugated blue outside, it seemed to be a former shipping container. He sniffed the air with the visible motion of a dog. Fried food. French fries, but the kind of French fry smell of oil that had sat out overnight.

James bent down and crept closer to the

office. Rapid-fire traffic reports spewed forth from a radio. A pair of feet leaned against the desk. The paperback cover of *30 Days to a New You* peeked over the boots. James straightened up and slouched, hoping the exaggerated gait would appear casual.

"Hey." James stood in the booth doorway. What else was he supposed to say?

Despite his surroundings, the man who dropped the paperback on the floor was immaculately groomed. He had a perfectly trimmed mustache and beard—the kind shaved so close to the skin it looks painted on.

James leaned over and scooped up the book. "Sorry to scare you, but I thought I should tell you I saw someone snooping around."

The painted-beard man set his booted feet down on the dusty floor of the booth. "What were they doing?"

Removing his hat, James scratched his head. "I don't know, but it looked suspicious, man. Thought I should tell someone." He pointed toward the water. "You might catch him if you go now. Right by the red container with the halfway-open door."

The man sighed, hitched up his pants, and walked toward the container at an un-hurried pace.

As James moved closer to the door of the booth, the painted-beard man spun round.

"Hey," said the man, "can you show me where?"

"Oh, I, ah, I need to get going—or my boss will get mad. You know how that goes."

The man snorted in empathy, turning back toward the container. As soon as he was out of sight, James hopped into the booth and scanned the walls. Candy wrappers littered the floor. An ancient computer sat on one end of the booth, and a file cabinet on another. Locked.

20

Shit. He fumbled in his pockets but couldn't find his pocketknife.

He stood there for a minute, closed his eyes, and remembered a lock-picking session with Nia. Paperclips. There must be a paperclip. A stack of papers sat on the desk so he flipped through them, hoping someone would have run out of staples and had to use a paperclip. The last packet of papers on the bottom held a rusted paperclip. Looked like the stack of papers hadn't been moved for at least a decade.

He quickly unbent the paperclip and jammed it into the file cabinet lock. It should be easy, he thought. It's just one of those cheapo old cabinets. He crouched down, closed his eyes, and tried to calm his fingers even as he jiggled the paperclip wire furiously in the lock.

Someone was speaking on the phone. Coming toward the booth.

Click. The file cabinet lock sprung open. James rummaged around inside the first drawer. Nothing. Paydirt! A mess of lanyards with badges—thank God they didn't have photographs—sat like a beautiful plate of blue spaghetti in the next drawer.

A dog barked. And then it barked again. Closer.

James tried to untangle the lanyards. As this was a futile task, he grabbed the entire bunch and stuffed them underneath his shirt. As he tilted his head up, he realized he was invisible from outside the booth.

But now the dog barked at the booth. Shit. Shit. Had the painted-beard man returned with a dog?

"Yeah, I've got him. He's in the booth." A muffled voice came closer.

Scanning every inch of the booth, James saw there was another door opposite the main door, but it had been painted shut.

Scissors. A pair hung from a nail in the wall. He grabbed them, opened them all the way and scraped at the paint furiously. Flecks sprayed everywhere, but it was having an effect. Sirens echoed in the distance. It wouldn't have anything to do with him, he told himself. There were sirens all the time.

Focus, James, focus, he said to himself.

The dog scraped at the door.

He pushed on the painted door and it opened, ever so slowly. Then, with one great push, he stamped his foot against the door and it busted wide open. He shot out of the other side of the tollbooth, heading for the closest container row. His joints creaked but he soon skidded round the corner. A dog barked. And it was getting closer.

He stood rooted to the spot for a moment. Deciding the best course of action would be to weave in and out of the containers back to the fence, he ran down the aisle, just as he heard the dog turn the corner.

He tripped. He had no idea why, but he just tripped and toppled over. The German Shepherd loped toward him, five feet away. James scrambled to his feet, clawing at the dirt. The dog grabbed his pantleg—the pantleg that had survived the encounter with the fence. James was on his feet now so in one great, jerking motion he ripped away his leg from the dog and ran like he had never run before.

After twists and turns through the Starburst candy-colored containers, he made it back to the chain-link fence. He scrambled through to the other side and bent over to catch his breath.

No sound. No dog. No painted-beard man.

As he stood back up, he realized Nia and Shanice were gone. Nowhere to be seen. He even poked his head inside the fence—after a good five minutes of waiting—to make sure they weren't there.

His stomach clenched and he felt like a fool. Was this a joke? Or a sick test? Hadn't he passed enough tests yet? Were they lying about why they needed the badges?

As he stood there, arms crossed, having his own little pity party, cursing the day he met Shanice, cursing his ex, and cursing his luck, a low rumble echoed behind him.

21

A shipping container truck pulled up next to him.

Though his body wouldn't move, James' mind raced with images of the painted-beard man and the dog.

The truck door opened, revealing a leg in purple jeans. He knew those purple jeans.

"Nia!" he cried.

She tipped her baseball hat at him and smiled.

"C'mon. Get in."

Shanice's hands rested against the steering wheel. She grimaced as James hopped into the truck.

"I see you survived. But it looks like your

pants didn't," she said in her driest tone possible.

With what he knew must be a self-satisfied grin, he pulled blue-laced lanyards from underneath his shirt.

"Yes!" Nia pumped her fist.

"I was followed, though. By a man." James paused and pointed at his shredded pant leg. "And a German Shepherd."

"I see." Shanice bit her lip and rubbed her chin. "You can't go back into the yard with those pitiful pants."

"Even if my pants were fine, it would be risky since they chased me."

"OK. Here's what we'll do. Nia and I will drive in. James, you must stay curled up in that little space behind the seat."

James eyed the cramped space between the seat and cab doubtfully.

"It's the only way. It'll seem odd if you stay in the truck when we enter the yard."

He nodded. "OK, since we're close to the entrance, I'll get into the back now." He yanked back the seat and crammed himself in.

"Ahh!" He stuck his hand underneath him, touching something cold and hard.

Metal.

A pair of bolt-cutters. "What the fuck? Why do we have these?"

"They always come in handy in these situations. Sorry—I forgot they were back there."

"I'll be bruised all over by tomorrow."

Nia and Shanice exchanged glances but said nothing. Shanice started the engine and they rumbled toward the entrance.

As they slowed to a halt, he heard someone say, "Which station?"

Shanice replied, "Tatsun. Pickup."

The containers whizzed by until Shanice hit the screeching brakes. All he could see was the sky and red containers labeled "Tatsun."

Shanice and Nia got out of the truck, but left the doors open.

"We're here for a pickup," said Shanice.

A low voice replied, "Where's your paperwork?"

Paper crinkled.

"Looks good," said the low voice. "Ah, wait a minute. This is dated last week. It's hard to see, but the one is a seven."

He heard a long, low growl. "I told that

fuck to get his paperwork straight, didn't I, Jamie?"

"You sure did. But he's an idiot."

"This is the second time this happened this morning. Let me text this guy to confirm, alright?"

"Sure," replied the low voice.

Shanice said, "I tried calling but he's not picking up. No text. Please don't send me away. We could both get fired because of this guy's stupidity."

James had never understood the expression "hemmed and hawed" until that moment. "Tell you what. Let's load the container onto the truck—you might get a text back from the guy by then."

"Great. Thanks, I really appreciate it."

After a great deal of rattling, scraping, and bumping, the container settled onto the truck. The doors were still open. Nia crawled into the truck and winked at James.

"I've got to tell off this guy off on the phone, OK?" Shanice said. "You don't want to listen to it, so let me get in the truck."

Shanice hopped in, closed the door, and stuck the keys in the ignition. She put the phone up to her ear as if she were talking to someone and waved her hands around. Nia leaned over, turned on the truck, and put it in gear. Shanice gripped the wheel, hit the gas, and they rocketed back just enough to make a three-point turn.

"Hey! Come back!"

Shanice made the three-point turn and sped away. James glanced behind them and saw a short, squat figure running after them. They turned to the left, leaving the irate figure behind.

"Won't he call the cops?" James wiped his brow.

Nia shook her head. "He'll be too embarrassed—he'd lose his job. Besides, Shanice left him a nice note with a nice fat payoff, didn't you?"

"Mmmhhh."

James now sat in an upright fetal position, watching Shanice maneuver the beast toward the exit. She rolled down the window and flashed her badge.

The gates opened and they were free.

"Have a seat." Abner pointed at a wicker chair on the terrace. The terrace overlooked the bay—Angel Island, Alcatraz, and the city skyline. Eucalyptus aroma mingled with the wisteria draped over the arbor in front. Lazy bumblebees buzzed about, drunk on sweet nectar.

"Tiburon is the place to be." James slouched back in his chair and folded his arms behind his head.

"Definitely in the summer, that's for sure." Abner pushed his sunglasses up his nose. "But I prefer winter in Corsica. We have a villa there."

"I bet you do. Someday I want one there,

too."

"Well, if you play your cards right, you might."

James produced a slow, slimy smile. He knew he had one after years working in real estate, but he had consciously been practicing it in the mirror over the past week.

Abner pulled his chair closer and popped an olive in his mouth. "Tell me how Girard can help us."

Staying in his relaxed position, James stared out at the bay. "I've figured out how to get around the planning permission process for an art installation at Juniper Downs—the place you want to revitalize."

"And you think the art will be good publicity?"

"Yeah, for sure. I sent you an email with a bunch of links to places like London, Hamburg, Stockholm, New York, and other cities where the developers hired artists to 'beautify' the property as they tear down the structures from before. It's like insurance against bad publicity—doesn't guarantee good coverage, but it protects against bad."

"I'm not worried about a random news story here and there—I just don't want other planning commissioners to get ahold of the story and make it their cause célèbre."

"Exactly. This will do it."

"What does Girard get out of it?" Abner paused. "Let me guess. He expects deals on other property."

"You got it. He has his eye on a few East Bay properties, and since it's outside San Francisco city limits, no one can say he has a conflict of interest."

"You mean he wants them for free?" Abner pushed down his sunglasses and stared at James.

"No, I think he wants, well, a substantial discount."

"I can arrange a discount if he can pull this off. But he knows there's no deal until it's finished, right?"

"He told me to tell you he wants two deals—one on the Richmond property and the other on the Oakland property. The Oakland property is non-negotiable, upfront. He wants half off. The Richmond deal will follow—once we pull off the installation."

"I need to sleep on it."

James looked down. A text popped up

from Shanice in reply to his earlier message: *Push once, but not twice.*

He slipped the phone into his pocket. "I'm supposed to have a phone meeting with Girard. What should I tell him? I'm in an awkward position."

"Should I talk to Girard myself?" Abner pushed back from the table.

James shrugged. "You could, but he wouldn't be happy. He wants to stay at a distance from you—in case word gets out."

Abner responded in a low growl. "Why would word get out?"

James held his hands up in mock surrender. "You know that leaks are always a possibility."

Abner shrank back in his chair, sending his jowls flapping. "I still need some time. Can you put off Girard till tomorrow morning? I'll text you with my decision by eight."

"Fair enough." James grinned.

Abner rubbed his hands together. "And now we can enjoy my wife's bouillabaisse."

23

James' stomach lurched as the elevator jerked upward. He gritted his teeth as the smell of pine air freshener became stronger in the enclosed space.

Nia put a hand on his arm. "Are you alright? You look like you're going to puke."

James shook his head, still staring at the ceiling.

The elevator finally stopped, with a sudden bounce. James stumbled out and leaned against a gray concrete pillar. He held up one hand.

"Quick—Nia—can you get that garbage can?" asked Shanice.

Shanice put the can in his hands. Miserable, James retreated to a dark hallway and soon felt better. Much better. He glanced up and saw a men's room. Grateful to be saved the embarrassment of presenting his garbage can to Nia and Shanice, he cleaned the can in the toilet and sink. Relieved, but still weak, he leaned against the sink and peered in the mirror at his ever-deepening lines on his forehead. Not for the first time that day, he wondered what the hell he was doing. Here he was, at Juniper Downs, completely out of place and feeling more useless than ever. He had joined the crew with the hope of revenge against Alana, and yet he couldn't see how that had anything to do with these apartments or this con.

The door swung open and a small man with a gray mustache and wool cap edged in on a walker. His eyes widened as he looked at James. Then he chuckled. "Your bathroom isn't working, either. Mine's been out a week. How about yours?"

As this was apparently a bravado contest, James thought it best to let him win. "Oh, mine's been out just one day. They said they'd fix it soon."

"When hell freezes over, young man." He

shuffled into a stall, pushing the door open with his walker.

James left the bathroom and inhaled the stale but slightly fresher air in the hallway.

Nia popped her head round the corner. "Feeling better?"

Still weak, James tried to put on a brave face. Especially as Shanice's crossed arms indicated slight impatience. "It must have been Abner Maxey's bouillabaisse. I don't think I'll be eating any seafood for a while."

"Should we leave you here while we see my auntie?" Shanice moved toward the next hallway. James realized he'd soon find out whether Shanice was actually Charisse when her auntie answered the door.

"No, no. I'm fine. Let's go."

A purple door numbered 34 stood around the corner.

Shanice banged on the door. "Auntie Didi is a little deaf," she said apologetically.

The shuffling of feet was followed by an elaborate clicking and clunking of locks.

"Sherry! Come in, come in." A tall, thin-boned woman in black leggings and a plain green dress led them into her cheery, yellow-tiled kitchen. James walked slowly, hoping to glimpse some family photo that might tell him more about Shanice. Photos covered the wall, but none of them stood out as significant.

Auntie Didi busied herself with a coffeepot and a tin of dried coffee crystals with a dust-encrusted top. Shanice put a hand on her shoulder. "Auntie, I'm afraid we can't stay. I just need to ask you a couple of questions and we'll be on our way."

Auntie Didi's shoulders slumped as she slid the tin back into the cupboard.

"But I'll be back soon for a longer visit. Don't you worry," Shanice said directly into her aunt's ear.

Didi threw up her hands. "You've forgotten your manners, Sherry. Aren't you going to introduce me to your boyfriend?"

Nia suppressed a giggle. James stiffened and ran a finger around his collar.

Shanice licked her lips as her hands flew in random directions. "Oh, ah, these are friends, Auntie." She then closed the cardigan around her tightly. James had never seen Shanice so discombobulated. "James is a work colleague and Nia is a friend's niece."

Didi's eyes slid from Nia to James. "But why are they here with you today?"

James crossed his arms. How was Shanice going to get out of this one?

"I told them about the developers who have been circling—"

"Just like sharks," said Didi.

"Yep," said Shanice. "Anyway, they wanted to see if they could help stop you losing your home."

Now Didi's eye movement over James was more rapid. "And how are they going to do that?"

Nia opened her mouth, glanced at Shanice, and then shut it.

Rather than answer her aunt, Shanice withdrew her phone and began to scroll. "Let me find the pictures."

"Are they nasty pictures of the developers?" Didi giggled as she leaned over her niece.

"Thankfully, they're not." Shanice held up the phone close to Didi's face. "Do you recognize this man?"

Didi's eyes widened and she sucked in her breath. "Oh, yes. We call him Mr. Sunglasses. Because he wears them on the back of his head every time he shows up."

James tried to move past Nia to see the phone, but he was stuck in the corner between the wall and the table.

"What do you know about him?" asked Nia.

"He's always poking around, saying he worries about our safety. I think he's been searching for problems with the building so he can say it's unsafe for us to live in it." Didi snorted. "This piece of junk has been unsafe since the day it was built, but nobody ever cared about that. You should have seen how it swayed in the 1991 earthquake! You know, the one where part of the Bay Bridge collapsed?"

They all shook their heads. James had remembered the TV footage from that awful day. His stomach began to turn over gently, warning of impending nausea.

Didi gripped the chair. "But whenever Mr. Sunglasses shows up, we just nod and say everything is fine. Then we try to get him out of the building as fast as we can."

"Shanice, can I see the phone? Who is Mr. Sunglasses?"

Shanice paused, looked at the phone, and sighed. She handed it to James.

James' mouth fell open. There was no mistaking it. It was Seth Hummel, his ex's lover.

———

"Put your back into it, James!" Esme flung a green paint glob at James' shirt.

"Hey!" he yelled back in mock anger. Instead of flicking paint at Esme, he did at Nia. That was a mistake, he thought, as Nia approached him with a whole can of purple paint. She held it over his head as Shanice said, "Children, now don't bother each other."

The crew stood back and surveyed their work. Not bad for a bunch of amateurs. Well, except for Nia. She wasn't an amateur. A colorful mural of a city street stood on one side of the container and a nature scene was on the other. Nia had painted the mural outlines the night before, and they had fun filling in the enormous paint-by-the-numbers project today. Though the abandoned lumberyard wasn't exactly an inviting location. Edie had figured out a way they could make it non-abandoned for a few days.

Nia leaned on her friend Quinn. "Pure artwashing. At its finest."

Quinn was a long and lean friend of Nia's, with close-cut hair and dimples.

Quinn drew a circle in the sand with the toe of their shoe. "So this rich dude is coming to see the mural and we're supposed to sell it to him?"

Shanice sighed. "Kind of. That's all you need to know. Let us do the talking. If he asks you about your life and where you live, you can tell him—no need to lie about any-thing, K?"

Quinn shrugged and nodded. They leaned against a wall and nibbled on a paint-brush, surveying their handiwork. "So what am I supposed to tell everyone at home? At Juniper Downs? I still don't see how this is going to stop them from tearing down the houses. My uncle is worried."

"You can tell them anything. But make sure to tell them no one will tear their houses down. Reassure them. Don't tell them they'll get cash, though. Not just yet. I can promise their homes are safe, but I can't promise about the money."

"Hey!" Shanice shrieked.

"It's just a mouse," cooed Nia.

"That was a rat," said Shanice. "You know how I feel about rodents."

Nia turned to James. "There was this one time we lost a mark because of Shanice's fear of rodents."

"Do tell." James smiled but then quickly became serious when he saw Shanice pull her jacket closer. He glimpsed a quivering lip. Interesting. Nia had hurt her pride. "I'm not a fan of rats, either."

Nia looked at the rat footprints left in the dust. "I love rats."

"Me too!" said Quinn.

"Can we leave the rats alone, please?" Shanice glanced at her phone. "Girard is coming soon. Edie and Miss Esme should hide in the office. And James and I need to change out of these clothes before he comes."

Edie and Esme ran into the office.

James was a few steps behind them when he heard an approaching car.

Shanice stiffened. "Shit. I guess we'll have to figure this out as we go."

A gleaming black Range Rover turned in through the gate. It came to a halt in a cloud of dust in front of the container.

Girard jumped out of the backseat. James peered at the driver. He didn't recognize the man but Girard often hired different drivers.

Dressed in his version of casual, Girard wore a green polo shirt, black jeans, and shoes that must have cost a mint. Both he and his driver wore aviators.

Shanice approached Girard, removing her sunglasses. Girard reciprocated. James took notes on this move—Shanice had told him she could get anyone to mirror her gesture. But it only worked when the person was uncomfortable—as Girard was, in this case.

"Thanks for making the trek out here." Shanice shook Fulton's hand. "You can see Belle's been busy. And this is her friend, Quinn, who's been helping out."

Girard shook Quinn's hand. "I see you've also been busy." He pointed at Shanice and James' paint-covered clothes.

James scrutinized Fulton's face. Fulton

raised his left eyebrow—a strangely unreadable gesture.

Shanice pulled off her paint-speckled sweater. "Oh, yes. James and I don't usually do this, but the painting crew had to work elsewhere today—so I asked James to pitch in."

"But are either of you painters?" Fulton's eyebrow rose a half-inch higher.

"Oh, no. Ah." James paused, catching himself before he said "Nia." He cleared his throat. "Belle painted the outline for us and we filled in with the paint. Like paint-by-the-numbers."

Girard let out a stream of air as his eyebrows went back to the resting position. "I get it." He put his hands on his hips and walked backward as he surveyed the container. "Well, it looks good. More or less what I pictured."

He clapped James on the back. "Can I talk to you for a minute over there?"

"Sure thing." James trotted after Girard.

"So what did Maxey say this morning?" Girard scrolled through his texts. "I didn't see any texts from you."

"That's weird." James shrugged. "Maxey

said the deal is on. The Oakland property is yours now and you'll get the Richmond one after we're through with the installation."

"Great. Well done, James. I'm sure there's a bonus—or something that won't break the ethics rules—coming your way."

A police siren wailed in the distance. They were on edge since several police cars had circled the abandoned yard. Some had slowed down in front—without their sirens on—but none had stopped. James felt his eyelid flinch with every pulse of the siren.

Girard was unconcerned by it. They walked back to Shanice, Nia, and Quinn.

"So, Jasmine, what's the deal? How do we compensate SanCul and the artists?" Girard gestured to Nia and Quinn. "You know my restrictions on this. I can't pay out of city funds."

Shanice put one foot in front of another and leaned forward. "Of course, Mr. Girard. We appreciate the sensitivity of the whole situation. That's why we have the Artists' Trust." She glanced at Nia. Nia gestured toward Quinn and they padded toward the mural. They dipped their brushes in blue and green and painted in a garden.

"The Artists' Trust is a fund we run to pay various artists' stipends for work like this. We don't pay them like it's a job or an award—just the stipend. And then we invest the funds. In socially responsible investment portfolios, of course." The corner of Shanice's mouth wiggled ever so slightly when she said this.

"Of course. I understand. So your goal is to pour as much money as possible into the Artists' Trust."

"Yes. Especially because we've found some creative accounting ways to avoid the usual problems with nonprofit status."

The words "creative accounting" worked like a dream on Girard. A faint, slow smile spread across his face.

"I like your style, Jasmine."

"Why thank you, Mr. Girard," she said in fake little-girl voice.

"I'm sure we can come to a satisfactory arrangement. How does one million sound?"

"Very generous. I know how much it will mean to the artistic community."

A flashing light spread across the shipping container as quickly as a virus in a day-care center.

24

———————

The cops.

Fulton's sly-fox smile had turned into a menacing leer.

"What the hell? Is this a setup?" Girard grabbed Shanice's arm. James felt confused for a minute—why would he grab Shanice's arm and not his? *Because you are trustworthy to him, you fool.*

Girard shook Shanice as the car approached, though they were still half hidden from sight by the office.

"Let me go! Get off. I had nothing to do with this. And I'm the one who should be worried in this situation." Shanice snatched her arm away and rubbed it.

"This better not be a setup, you—" He left the last word unsaid as the cops got out of the car. Though they were in a conventional cop car, their uniforms were different. Almost paramilitary—boots with green pants and shirt.

One with a soft green baseball cap approached first. He nodded at James. "Officer Sanchez. This is Officer Malinowsky." He pointed at the small blond white woman with pointy vampire teeth. James stood like a mouse before a snake.

"Oh, ah, hello, Officer. How can we help you?"

As Sanchez stood ramrod-straight, Malinowsky meandered away. James' palms were wet now, he was glad he didn't have to shake hands. At least Malinowsky walked toward the container rather than the office.

"We had a report of a shipping container stolen from the Oakland shipyards. We're searching abandoned places like this lumberyard."

"Really? Sounds like a difficult job—to steal a container, I mean. Jasmine can tell you about our mural project." James lifted his chin in Shanice's direction.

"Yes, Officer Sanchez, I'm director of San-Culture Consulting and Leadership, and I can assure you we procured this container by legal means." Shanice handed him a business card from her back pocket. Damn, the woman was always prepared.

Sanchez's chiseled face remained impassive. He flipped the business card over a few times in his fingers and tapped it against his cheek.

Malinowsky bent down and peered at the bottom corner, where they had painted over the tracking number for the container.

"Hey, Sanchez." Malinowsky waved at her partner. "Check this out." She took out a penknife and scraped away the paint.

"Excuse me! You can't do that—it's our private property. Do you have a warrant?"

Malinowsky glared at Shanice. "No, we don't. But do you have something to hide? After all—it's just a blob of paint."

"A blob of paint?!" Nia ran up to Malinowsky. "A blob of paint?"

Shanice put a hand on Nia's shoulder. "It's the only way they'll go away. And I'll help you repaint it."

Nia stood with her arms crossed, saying

nothing. Shanice gave a nod to Sanchez and Malinowsky. "Go ahead, but please don't scrape off more than is necessary."

After an eternity, the paint scrapping revealed a ten-digit number. Sanchez stood up. "This isn't the container we've been searching for. We'll be on our way." He walked back to the car. Nia glared after the retreating Malinowsky, who didn't bother to wave or say goodbye.

James reflected it was odd Girard had said nothing during the entire exchange. He stood there, transfixed. James thought Girard might try to pull the "I'm a planning commissioner so leave us alone" card, but he just stared at the dirt.

As the police car drove off, Girard ran toward the office.

"Where are you going?" Shanice followed him.

"I need the bathroom."

They stared at each other in a moment of slow motion where no movement seemed fast enough.

James covered his eyes as Girard reached the door.

Girard pushed the door open and disappeared inside.

Everyone held their breath. The toilet flushed. Girard came out, his white face now translucent.

He swaggered over, a gesture that clashed with his clearly uncomfortable, bloodless face. "So that's it, right? I guess it's a good thing we got this whole container business cleared up right now rather than later." He clapped a hand on James' shoulder. "And we're sure the planning code will allow the shipping containers on the grassy area in front of the apartment buildings?"

James nodded. "Yep. I checked, double-checked, and then rechecked with three different code specialists—though I made it vague enough they won't be able to trace anything to me."

Girard turned back toward Shanice. "Consider the check already in the mail."

"Check? Ah, we deal in cash, Mr. Girard. Not that anything will go wrong, but you understand it's better if this isn't traceable."

"Of course. Thing is, I've never had to do anything like this before. With cash, I mean."

Girard stared at Quinn. Quinn said nothing but glared back at him.

"Well, I'll go to the bank. Though it might put us behind schedule."

Girard poked James in the ribs. "I'm kidding! I've got the cash ready. Just wanted to see your faces. No problem at all."

25

———

Shanice rubbed her temples as they sat in a circle in the living room. Rain pattered against the windows. The cat meowed.

"Edie, could you feed Opal?"

Edie crunched on a potato chip, wiped her fingers and padded off into the kitchen, luring the crying cat behind her.

Esme patted Shanice's knee. "What's wrong? You look like you have a migraine."

Nia stretched and folded her legs into a lotus position on the couch. "Everything's worked out—we're so close. We should get ready to celebrate!"

Shanice munched absently on one of Edie's jalapeño chips, only to have her eyes alight a minute after. "Water, please!" She scrambled for a water bottle on the table.

"Ah. That's much better. Everything's going too well—it's bothering me."

"Oh yes, the grifter's curse." Esme's voice deepened. "The curse inevitably happens when you become a first-class grifter. You're so good that things go to plan, but you mistrust the plans because they're going so smoothly."

Shanice slammed the table. "Bam! That's it. Everything's going so smoothly—minus a few hiccups—so it's making me nervous."

"The trick is to take apart which part is your experience of having things go wrong and which part is your gut instinct telling you something is wrong."

"It might help if you said it aloud." Opal jumped on Edie's lap. Their tiff had been patched up.

Shanice leaned against the fireplace. "Good idea. I'll try it because I'm getting lost in my head." She surveyed each of them. "And you should tell me if your gut tells you something's wrong, OK?"

They nodded.

"Let's start with the big picture. Everything is going too well, too smoothly."

"Such as?" Nia munched on a chip.

"Well, we could start with money. First, James gets Maxey to agree to the one-two-punch plan of the deals before and after the art installation." Shanice winked at James. "No offense to you, but it just seemed too smooth."

James blew on his nails. "That's because I used my considerable powers of charm."

A pillow sailed across the room and hit his head. Nia chuckled and he chuckled back.

His smile faded. "Go on, I know what you mean—no offense taken."

"So there's that, and then there's Girard's weird behavior today."

"You mean not freaking out about the cops—or trying to use his influence?" Nia wiped her oily fingers on the handkerchief she always carried with her.

"Exactly. Both of those together. On top of it, he's completely fine with the use of cash."

"Well, he's from New Jersey. Not exactly

the most incorruptible place." Esme gave them a wry smile.

"True. But it makes me even more nervous. The fact he's a Jersey developer means at the very least he knows some of the tricks of the trade. In that case, why wouldn't he be more nervous?"

"But he has been nervous. You all haven't seen it, since it happens when it's just the two of us. Besides, he probably thinks he has to act a certain overconfident way in front of you all." James swiped the bag of chips from Nia.

"What do you mean, you all?" Nia grabbed the bag back.

"I mean, ah, women." His cheeks became hot.

Shanice waved away his comment. "OK, let's put aside Girard for a minute. How about what happened at the party?"

"You mean with the other commissioners?"

"Yep. I know we've already discussed Maggie's impeccable timing, but it's worrying me even more."

"Hmmm . . ." Esme smoothed her skirt.

"So how does this add up? Just a bunch of strange coincidences or is there a pattern?"

"I can't see a pattern." Shanice spun around toward Edie. "What about you and Girard—has that gone anywhere? Is he still texting you?"

Edie scrolled through her phone. "He's still at it. But I can't put him off much longer. The pressure is on, and well, he thinks I'm a tease—because I am."

"Ooo, you are such a tease." Nia giggled.

What was that comment about? James was confused, as usual.

Edie tucked her hair behind her ear. "There is something else that's weird, though, about Girard. Have you noticed he has an accent?"

"That's it!" Shanice jumped up and down. "He has an accent! And it isn't a Jersey accent."

Edie smiled. "I couldn't place it at first, but there were a few words he used like 'car park' instead of 'parking lot' that weren't wrong, but struck me as strange choices at the time."

James scratched his head. "You're right. Now I remember him using the phrase 'full stop' instead of 'period.' I think my subconscious must have marked it as possibly a patrician Boston accent. You know, like he was born in Boston but grew up in Jersey."

"Did he tell you where he was born?" Nia stood near Shanice in a yoga tree pose. Then she dropped into downward dog.

"He supposedly was born in New Jersey. His name does sound, well, fancy. Kind of like a British aristocrat. He said his mother thought he would become a great man so she gave him a grand name."

"Or become an aristocratic serial killer," murmured Esme.

"Shit." Shanice tapped the back of her head on the fireplace ever so slightly. "Does it mean anything, though? There might be a perfectly good reason why he's hiding it."

"Maybe, but it seems weird given the other patterns we've noticed." Edie stroked Opal.

Esme held up her hands. "Let's not get carried away. The truth is, anything can happen in a long con. Everyone has secrets, and everyone lies. That means we naturally —and sometimes subconsciously—pick up on those secrets and lies. Nothing you all have said seems to point to any major problems."

Esme's phone buzzed. She held up a finger. "That will be Girard's phone call to Maxey."

James' jaw dropped. "What do you mean?"

Esme peered at James over her reading glasses.

"When I had my fainting—what's the old-fashioned term for it? Oh yes, when I had my 'fainting spell' at the party, I got access—temporarily—to Girard's phone. I set up a way to record any conversations between him and Maxey, should they be on that phone."

"And this is the first time Maxey and Girard have spoken on the phone. Right now."

26

Esme pressed the Bluetooth speaker button. The crackling noise of a bad phone call filled the room.

Everyone looked around as if a higher power had entered the room.

"Maxey. We need to talk," said Girard's voice.

"Mmmm . . ." Maxey sounded like he was drinking something. "Go on."

"What's James Bowman told you about this whole artwashing plan?"

"We'll install the painted containers on the grass in front of the apartments. Good publicity for us and you get something in return, too."

"But the cops showed up when I visited the container mural this morning. They were searching for a stolen shipping container."

"And?" Now Maxey was crunching on something.

"Well, they didn't find the stolen container, but it made me suspicious of the plan."

"I'm sure you've done your own homework on them. And everything seems aboveboard. Besides, there's always risk in these sorts of plans, isn't there?"

A long pause ensued. Loud, crinkling plastic echoed in the room.

"I don't know," said Girard. "Something's off. Something about those women—Jasmine and Belle."

"Now you're just being racist, Girard," chuckled Maxey.

"Fuck you," said Girard. "But how long have you known Bowman?"

"Ah, probably five years or so. Good guy. A bit clueless sometimes, but a good guy."

James saw slight smirks on everyone's faces.

"Well, I want insurance on this plan," said Girard.

"What did you have in mind?"

"I want the Richmond deal up front—along with the Oakland deal."

Loud sucking noises came from the recording. Sounded like Maxey had a hard candy rolling around in his mouth.

"If you think there's something fishy going on, wouldn't the Richmond deal make it worse?"

"It would prove you're not up to something, Maxey."

"Now wait a minute, Girard," said the voice, rising in volume. "Bowman approached me. Not you or whatever the arts consulting firm is."

A long pause again. "You say Bowman approached you?"

James' throat went dry.

"Mhmm . . . Said he had a deal I'd be interested in."

"Well, he approached me, too. I mean, he got a job in my office. This is getting weird, Maxey. Smells like rotten fish."

"Now you've told me that, I have to wonder."

"Bowman asked me to host a gathering so we could meet each other," said Girard.

"OK, if you're right, then what do we do? I know you're from Jersey and all, but we don't bury bodies out here as easily as you do back there."

"That's not exactly what I've heard," said Girard, "but I didn't have any violence in mind anyway. Not my style. And I gather by the way you operate, not the way you do, either."

"Hell, no. I stay away from that shit. I've seen too many developers go down that road. It's how they end up in prison—not for the violence, but because it exposes their creative accounting practices," said Maxey.

"So what are we going to do?"

"We shouldn't talk on the phone about this. Let's meet in person," said Maxey.

"Good idea. Where and when? My calendar is pretty open today."

"Clarissa's at one. In Noe Valley."

"I'll be there."

A dial tone rung out. Shanice switched off the speaker on her phone.

"Fuck, fuck, fuck." Edie leapt around the room.

"Watch your mouth, young lady." A slow smile spread across Esme's face.

"It's actually good news." Shanice tapped her phone against her lips.

"So I take it it's time to get dressed up to go to lunch!" Nia clapped her hands together with glee.

Shanice grinned. "You're so extra, Nee-Nee."

27

A half-hour later, they hurried into the car amid a downpour.

Edie brushed raindrops off the silver sleeve of her immaculate suit. "This is cozy, isn't it?"

"Except for the driver." Shanice growled as a semi passed them, spraying them with so much water they lost visibility for a second.

Nia turned her head toward the backseat. "Have any of you noticed the gray BMW following us? It's been there since we got on the freeway."

Shanice adjusted the rearview mirror and shook her head. "No, I haven't noticed it, but it's not surprising given this rain. There's so many ruts in the pavement I'm focused on not hydroplaning."

And true to her word, they hit a large pool of water. Shanice loosened her grip on the steering wheel and the trouble soon passed.

Esme, James, and Edie turned their heads in unison.

"Now you mention it, I noticed the car—if it's the same one—following us before we got on the freeway." Edie turned her head toward the front of the car.

"I didn't see it, but I wasn't looking. Besides, I don't have my glasses." Esme cackled.

"Miss Esme, you love playing up being old, don't you?" Nia turned and grinned. "Those reading glasses are just an act. You like to peer down your nose at people to make them feel uncomfortable."

"Don't disrespect your elders, Miss Nia." Esme's hat was so large they had to clear out all of the junk from the trunk to make sure it arrived at their destination unscathed. They had tried to talk Esme out of her outfit, worrying it would draw attention to themselves, but she insisted the hat would hide her identity perfectly.

Shanice had told James to dress in a waiter's outfit. In this case, she knew the restaurant and knew the waiters wore black jeans and black dress shirts. He had already spilled coffee all over his jeans, but fortunately they were black.

James twisted his head behind him. "Could you turn on the back wiper? Then maybe we can see who is inside the car if they get close enough."

"I would have turned it on already but it's stuck."

James rolled down his window and peered out as they were whipping across the bridge. He gasped in the cold air. The raindrops stung.

Edie, who sat in the middle, pulled on James' shoulder. "Don't be an ass, James," she said as she pulled him back inside. "The art of the con is just that—an art. Art is subtle."

Nia snorted. "A loud show isn't subtle, Edie."

"OK, OK, but you know what I mean. You can't stick your head out like that." Edie turned toward the disheveled James. "They might recognize you."

"I get your point, but still, the driver can't see me since I'm on the other side of the car."

"He has a point." Esme looked at James with new appreciation. "Though if the driver can't see you, how will you see the driver?"

James didn't have an answer. He changed the subject. "So are you going to lose the gray BMW, Shanice?"

"It will be obvious if they're really following us once we get off the main road and head toward the valley."

Sure enough, as they split off from the main artery into the heart of the city, the gray BMW sped past them.

An audible sigh fogged up the windows.

"Sorry." Shanice twisted various knobs. "Nothing's working on the car today—including the defroster. Can you all open your windows?"

"I'm not opening mine," said Esme. "You've got another thing coming if you think I'll damage my outfit with all that rain."

Everyone else opened the windows. James breathed in eucalyptus and a hint of sea air as they took the scenic route near Golden Gate Park. They drove through Outer Sunset and looped around toward Noe Valley.

"There's Clarissa's." Nia pointed at a bustling corner restaurant with high ceilings and large windows.

"We'll be late if we have to keep circling for parking." Shanice craned her neck toward Edie in the back. "I think it's time for the old parking trick."

Edie rubbed her hands together. "Well, there's certainly no shortage of rich people's cars to choose from."

"What are you going to do?" James' stomach flipped.

Nia giggled. Esme gave out her low, raspy laugh from the front seat.

Edie patted him on the shoulder. "Watch and learn." The car came to a halt in front of a five-minute loading zone. "You can observe from the sidewalk."

"Go on, James. It's good for you to observe Edie in action. Plus, it will get you in the mood for your shenanigans."

Edie slid out of the car and James followed. She opened the trunk, pulled out a small bag, and disappeared into the car. When she emerged, she had on a navy uniform, hat, and badge. She winked at James and sauntered up the block, peering at each car.

Edie came to a halt in front of a blue Tesla. She rapped on the window with her knuckle. The window slid down. She touched her cap and the car began to move.

Genius. Except James saw the telltale little car of a real parking attendant trundling slowly toward them.

"Get down!" hissed James. Edie crouched down behind a large black Range Rover.

A gaggle of men hovered near Edie as she hid behind the car. "Hey! You!"

By their articulate exclamations, James could tell they had already had a few Sunday mimosas. The sweet, acrid smell of alcohol wafted toward James.

"Enjoy your job, don't you?" said one of the men, wobbling closer toward her. Edie stood up, bending over a little so the enormous car still hid her from vision. James moved closer.

"Fuck off, asshole," she said to him.

"Ooooo!" said another one of the crowd.

They moved in closer toward Edie. James moved in behind them.

Edie dialed her phone. "Yes, requesting backup now." Edie carefully annunciated each word.

That was all it took. The instigator moved on unsteadily, followed by his friends.

The little parking attendant car trundled slowly past them. By the time Edie walked over to James, Shanice had already maneuvered their car into the space vacated by the Tesla.

"Never a dull moment."

28

James' phone read 12:30. Plenty of time to get settled in before everyone else arrived.

Even though it was Sunday brunch, the line was short. Shanice requested a booth well away from the restrooms as a precaution against Girard or Maxey spotting them. She also found out how many waitstaff worked there. James would easily go unnoticed, especially on a busy day like Sunday.

After they settled themselves in a gleaming red booth, James came over to them, pad and pen in hand.

"Good afternoon, ladies." James gave them a little bow.

Nia had already secured a mimosa,

which she now tipped in salute toward James.

He leaned in. "Tell me what I need to do one more time." His hands were even more clammy than they had been in the car.

Shanice's head appeared from behind Esme's enormous hat. She'd left it on because there was nowhere to store it.

"Figure out who is serving Girard and Maxey. Follow that person around, without making yourself noticeable. Then, once you see their tray ready to go out, put the listening dot underneath a coffee cup saucer, or whatever might be convenient. That's it."

"OK, got it." He took a deep breath.

Nia, Shanice, Edie, and Esme all gave him a broad smile like he was a small child who had performed an adorable feat. But he'd take the encouragement in any form he could get at this point.

He stood near the entrance, pouring glasses of water and rearranging silverware on tables that had already been set. Just as he was about to run out of made-up tasks, Abner Maxey's voice boomed across the restaurant.

"We have a reservation. Maxey for two. In

a corner. Your quietest table, though I realize it's difficult at this time of day."

Girard and Maxey's suits made them stand out among the relaxed and casual dress of everyone else, despite the fact this was an upscale restaurant.

A young man who appeared to be no older than twelve ambled up to them.

"I'll have an extra-large latte, your sausage omelets, and a strawberry crêpe for dessert." Maxey licked his lips.

No wonder the man resembled a bulldog.

Girard handed the menu to the server. "I'll have green tea, your side of fruit, and steel-cut oatmeal, please."

James trundled after the twelve-year-old to the kitchen.

Shit. He had forgotten the drinks would be assembled separately from the food. This was more complicated than he expected.

Rather than go into the kitchen, he stood by the coffee bar, rearranging spoons. The ticket moved closer and closer to the purple-haired barista. After what seemed to be agonizing hours watching the milk foam, the drinks were complete.

James gestured to the barista. "Oh, ah, I'll take these. Too complicated to explain." He whisked the drinks away. Yes! He was home free. Now he just had to set them down and put the dot on the saucer. On the bar near the kitchen entrance, he stuck on the listening dot Esme had given to him.

"Excuse me, but aren't those my drinks?"

Adrenaline coursed through his veins. He turned around to see, to his relief, the server assigned to Fulton's table. For a moment, he had been certain it was Girard's voice.

"Here, give them to me before they get cold." The server now looked like a twelve-year-old crossed with a fluffy white sheepdog, with long bangs in his eyes.

"Right. Here you go," said James, before he could think of any way to stall. He placed the drinks on the server's tray, already laden with a strawberry crêpe so delicious-looking it made James forget his troubles for a split second.

As the sheepdog trundled off toward Girard's table, James stood there with his hands on hips, thinking. Then staring. Staring at the bowls of sugar at the bar. He scooped one up and stuck the dot on the underside, in what he considered to be a smooth move.

Sheepdog returned, tray empty.

"Hey—would you take this to the table with the strawberry crêpe? That big guy said he wanted sugar and I forgot all about it."

"Why don't you?" The sheepdog blew upward at his bangs.

"Would you do it for me? I spilled something on the tall guy and I don't want to add insult to injury."

"Thanks for jacking up my tip, asshole." The sheepdog had an advanced vocabulary for a twelve-year-old.

"My pleasure." James whipped off the apron tied around his waist. "I quit!" He threw down his apron on the bar, spun on his heel and marched into the kitchen, feeling like a million bucks. He had always had a secret desire to have a dramatic quitting scene. This con business could be quite fun, once you got past the nervousness.

As he got lost in his character part in the kitchen, he realized he needed to get back to the table to hear the conversation. He located his bag in the backroom, tore off his dress shirt to reveal a *Star Wars* T-shirt featuring Yoda, put on a baseball cap, and walked out the back.

As he made his way through the crowd into the restaurant, he pulled down his cap as he saw Girard rising from the table, presumably to go to the bathroom.

They were neck and neck now, but the large person behind them was pushing him along with a force he was unable to stop. Girard stood next to him, and would surely turn to look at him.

Girard spun around.

James' heart stopped.

29

———————

"James! What a coincidence!" A Joker-like smile popped onto Fulton's face.

They shook hands. Girard gripped James' hand just a second too long.

"Are you meeting someone?" Girard's head swiveled around. Someone bumped into him.

"Excuse me," said someone behind him.

"C'mon." Girard piloted James toward the bar near the kitchen. James' arms and legs moved, but stiffly, like an automaton. He pulled down his cap, hoping it would somehow prevent Girard from seeing the crew in the booth. "Where's Evie?" Girard popped up his head. James froze.

"I don't see her." Girard continued the monologue.

How could he not see her? Was Esme's hat really that big?

James rotated around. The booth was now occupied by a family with three screaming children. Where had they gone? His shoulders slumped in relief.

James pulled out his phone from his back pocket and turned it on. "No clue. She was supposed to meet me here. Must have got caught up in something."

"Hmmm . . . yes, caught up might be the right word." Girard stared absently at his own phone.

"What do you mean?" James did his best to infuse his question with an undertone of danger.

"Oh, nothing. You know how it is on Sunday mornings. Everything ambles along. It is strange you two don't live together after a year, though. Do you think the relationship is headed anywhere?"

James removed his cap and ran his fingers through his hair. "To be honest, I don't know. She's well, hot and cold. And it's constant. The minute I think it's over, she gets all lovey-dovey. But then she won't answer my calls."

"Women. My Myra. Well. You know. We've been together, what, twenty years? It's comfortable."

"Mmmh . . ." James still stared at his phone.

Girard chuckled. "Looks like you are willing her to text you."

"Well, you wouldn't be too far wrong." He put away his phone, crossed his arms, and leaned against the bar. "So what are you doing here? Brunch with Myra?"

"No . . . not exactly." Girard paused. "Here about business. With Abner Maxey."

"*Really*?" James pulled a long face. "On a Sunday? You really should take time off work."

"Actually, it's about the business proposition we're all involved in." Girard sighed. "I'll be honest. I'm not entirely sure these arts consulting people are aboveboard, if you know what I mean."

"Well, the whole thing is hardly what you'd call aboveboard." James stared hard into his eyes. "I mean, it's not illegal, but it's not strictly ethical, either."

Girard stiffened.

James punched him in the arm. "Just kidding, man. Chill out. It's all good. But I understand if you want to tie up loose ends."

Fulton's shoulders inched downward. He clapped James on the shoulder. "Since you're here—and the lovely Evie isn't—why don't you join us at our table?"

"Oh, I couldn't. I mean, I don't want to interrupt."

"No, no. I insist." Little specks of spittle appeared on his lips when he said the word "insist."

Even if James had said no, he had little choice in the matter as Girard had already pushed him forward toward the table. Maxey, who was so engrossed in his strawberry crêpe that he had a bit of whipped cream on his nose, glanced up and dropped his fork. Recovering quickly, he rose from the table and grinned.

"James! What a coincidence."

"That's what I said, Maxey." Girard settled back into his own chair. He crossed his legs and arms and leaned against the back of the chair, as if he were ready to judge a rather dubious entry to a dog and pony show.

"Join us." Maxey pulled a chair without any effort from the next table. "Just finishing my breakfast. Can we get you anything?" He glanced around the room, presumably searching for a server.

"Thanks, but I'll wait." James glanced at his phone again.

"James has been stood up by Evie." Girard said this with rather more malicious pleasure than was called for, thought James.

"Shame. But I'm glad you're here, James." Maxey licked his spoon. "I have a proposition for you. And though I haven't talked about it with Girard, I bet he'll be interested too."

"Go on." James folded his hands in his lap. He stared at the table. The detritus from breakfast still littered the tabletop, but the sugar bowl had vanished. But so had Girard's meal, so it wasn't too unexpected.

"To be honest with you, neither I nor Girard are entirely satisfied with our little deal —if you can call it that. We've been in business long enough to know when something doesn't pass the smell test."

"Funny you should say it," said James. "I woke up at two in the morning with the sense something wasn't right. It wasn't like I had any idea what it was—it was just a feeling."

Maxey shot a glance at Girard. Girard blinked.

"That's it. Neither of us can point to exactly what's wrong."

"I've got it." Girard untangled his arms and legs and leaned over the table. "Too many coincidences."

James' Adam's apple glided down his throat, but became stuck halfway. The half-discarded sausage rind on Maxey's plate suddenly became nauseating.

"Such as?" James couldn't think of anything to say to stall. As if it mattered at this point.

"Well, there's the coincidence this morning." Girard smoothed down his linen napkin on the table. He waved his hand. "But it's common enough, I suppose."

"It's relationships." Maxey took a sip of his third latte.

"Yes! Too many coincidental relationships."

James leaned back. "You mean the whole Belle-Jasmine connection, and then the Jasmine connection to what you needed at a particular time?"

"Precisely. Glad you see what we see." Girard gently tapped his butter knife on the table.

"So what are you going to do?" James looked wide-eyed from one man to another.

Girard pulled up his chair and blew a puff of air across James' cheek. "No. The question is what are *you* going to do?"

30

———

"I'd like a Bloody Mary." James glanced over his shoulder at the server. Thank God it wasn't the sheepdog. He must have moved on by now.

He turned back to Girard and Maxey. "What did you have in mind?" Desperately seeking a prop, he grabbed the water pitcher and swiped a clean glass from a nearby table. He gulped down the water.

Girard leaned in. "We need to protect ourselves against this arts consulting thing. Since they're taking our money with nothing in return, we need to set them up to ensure we get our money back—"

"And expose them along the way." Maxey rubbed his hands together.

James blinked. Rapidly. Unable to process the information, he couldn't figure out what to say or do next. If he went to the bathroom, they'd suspect he might phone Shanice. He must stay put and hope the combination of healthy tomato juice, celery, and vodka would fuel his brain.

Bless the service in this place. An enormous Bloody Mary—more like gazpacho than a cocktail—stood in front of him.

"So you're saying we do the deal, but then expose them?" asked James.

"Mmmhhh . . ." Girard tapped the knife again on the table. "We give them the money. Then we call the cops?"

Maxey waved his hand. "Won't work. Besides, they'll say we gave them the money voluntarily—and they might have proof. And once the cops get involved"—he pointed a latte-foam-covered spoon at Girard —"the cops will poke around our business. And neither of us needs that headache."

"This brings us back to Bowman." Girard gave his knife a rest.

James munched casually on a stick of celery.

"We still want the job done. And it has to be done correctly. Can you guarantee that?" Girard laced his fingers together and pointed at James.

"How can I guarantee it?"

"By following them and keeping as close as you can. I'll give you the money. Jasmine and company should be satisfied, since you'll be nearby at all times with the money. You only pay them once the job is done."

"What do I get out of it?"

"Well, I can't give you a direct cut because it'll be traced to me—or Maxey—so you'll have to be happy with a promised future favor on a piece of land."

"Fair enough," said James. "But what happens if something goes wrong? Do I take the money and run?"

"Yep, but don't even think you can just vanish. You should know better than that. If you or Jasmine get any ideas, I have *friends* who'll pay you a visit," he said, letting his butter knife fall on the table with a clunk.

———

JAMES BLINKED in the sunlight outside Clarissa's. He fumbled for his sunglasses as Girard and Maxey lumbered out of the restaurant. Just in time, he slid them on. So exhausted he couldn't pretend anymore, he didn't want to give either of them a chance to look directly into his eyes.

Maxey's bulldog head peered up at him. "We'll be in touch. Don't go all soft on us."

Arms crossed, Girard nodded. Unlike Maxey, he was tall enough to gaze into James' eyes. Thank God for sunglasses. "Remember, I hired you for a reason."

Maxey and Girard nodded and split off in different directions. James crossed the street. He had to clear his mind. Even though his crew was nowhere in sight, he was sure they'd pick him up soon.

His phone had two messages:

We'll pick you up outside.

Where are you?

James replied: *Meet me in 10 minutes in the alley.*

Ten minutes to think. The weak sun warmed his back as he strolled aimlessly near the restaurant. The conversation with Girard and Maxey hadn't been overheard by the crew because the sugar bowl listening device had disappeared. So Shanice and company knew nothing about Girard and Maxey's proposal.

Turning the corner, James jogged to the end of the block. It would clear his mind. When he arrived at the end he was even more muddled. If he followed Girard and Maxey's plan, they would surely attack the crew—and possibly himself. But if he didn't go along with their plan, one of their underlings would undoubtedly beat him up. While James considered himself a brave person, he avoided physical pain. Despite a few scrapes in school, he'd never suffered anything serious. And when he'd been down and out after his divorce, he narrowly escaped a few barroom brawls. Now he'd need to face up to his fear.

A ringing noise made him look up. Dammit, his tinnitus was acting up again. Must be the stress. As he gulped the fresh air, he saw the black Mercedes rolling toward the curb. Must be the crew. Just in time. He had decided.

Thud.

James banged the ceiling of the car.

"Those bastards. How can they think they'll get away with this?"

"This'll sound sanctimonious," Shanice said as she turned off Mission Street. "But they get away with it every day, twenty-four-seven."

"Yes, but it's so in your face!" James waved his hands in front of him in disbelief.

Silence from the backseat.

"OK." James sighed. "Rant over. So what did you hear when the listening device sat on the table?"

"They said what you'd expect." Esme gave out a raspy cough-laugh. "They didn't trust us. Didn't think Black people could run a successful consulting firm, etcetera, etcetera, etcetera."

"They said that?" James twisted toward Esme.

Esme gave him the side eye and cleared her throat. "The point is they don't trust us, and we have to figure out a way out of this—and still hit the original goal."

"Why are we stopping?" Nia leaned forward. They came to a halt in front of a warehouse in the Bayview neighborhood.

"Sunday is a great time to run particular errands," Edie called from the backseat.

"Oh no." James saw Nia shake her head. "Not me, not here, not today. I don't want to get mixed up in your errands, Edie. I know what kind of errands you run."

James saw Edie smile in the rearview mirror. "C'mon, Nia. I know how much you like chocolate truffles."

"Did someone say chocolate truffles?"

31

Shanice laughed. "I better get some of those! I like caramels the best, remember, Edie?"

"Don't worry. We'll get plenty."

"I'll stay with the car." Shanice turned around to face the backseat. "Edie—this is your show. Tell us what to do."

Edie clambered over Nia and got out of the car. She slipped into the back alley and returned after a few minutes. James unrolled his window and she leaned in. "There's a van in the alley we'll be borrowing temporarily."

"What do you mean?"

Esme tapped James on the shoulder. "Hush. You ask too many questions."

"The van is ready to go, so Nia will drive

it when we leave. Esme and Nia will go in the van since it's a two-seater and Shanice, James, and I will leave in this car." Edie pulled a wisp of hair from behind her ear. "Now c'mon. Follow me."

Esme hopped in the van, while Edie, Nia, and James approached the padlocked door in the alley. After Edie liberated the door from its lock, they crept inside the warehouse. The smell of chocolate overwhelmed him. So thick he thought he could break off a piece of the air and pop it in his mouth. Though he'd never had a sweet tooth, his eyes goggled at the stack of gold-wrapped bars in the corner.

Large burlap bags full of cocoa beans stood near them as they entered. As they moved on through the factory, they moved past red-metal vats and long runways of conveyer belts. The warehouse was dark, so they turned on their phone lights, flashing on gold and silver whenever the lights hit a chocolate bar stack.

Edie pointed at a small office near the front. Nia shone her phone on the lock while Edie stuck a wire into the bolt. Clunk. Edie waved them inside.

"Holy mother of . . ." Nia put a hand over James' mouth.

The office was not an office, but a temperature-controlled storage room for the chocolate. Every inch of the room glittered with gold and silver wrappers. Edie disappeared and returned with three handcarts. They stacked the precious cargo on each of the carts and made at least five trips out to the alley and back.

Edie jumped in the van and arranged the chocolate bars.

James watched her shove the stacks of bars near the back. "Are we going to compensate the factory?"

"I had Nia haul off their rejects, which probably would have gone in the dumpster. You could say we did the company a favor. But yes, we'll leave them compensation." Edie pulled out a large padded envelope from her bag and handed it to James. "Put the envelope in the storage room."

"Why didn't we just buy their chocolate if we planned to pay anyway?"

"Sometimes you're like a small child who asks 'why' all day, aren't you?" She sat on her haunches, rearranging the bars around her.

A 'Mmmhhhh' came from Esme in the front seat. Edie turned around and handed Esme a chocolate bar. "Well, I don't mind if I do," he heard her say, followed by the telltale noise of crinkling paper.

Edie looked contrite. "We need the chocolate, but we don't need a paper or digital trail. For an order this size, they'd keep a record."

He nodded and padded back into the warehouse. Just as he was thinking the security system was rather lax, a scraping, then rattling, noise came from the front of the warehouse.

A beam of light hit him as the front door opened. He saw a silhouette of a large person in the doorway. The figure marched toward him.

None of the vats or machinery provided enough cover, so James crouched down and crawled along the floor.

The footsteps sped up. Either the floorboards were weak or the person was very large.

James dove into the office and hid behind a stack of bars.

But the door was still open.

A flashlight beam spun wildly around outside the small room.

He must close the door. Flattening himself on the floor, which was covered in a thin film of cocoa dust and dirt, he wriggled toward the door. A sharp pain shot up through his groin. His mouth opened to scream, but somehow his body had enough self-preservation instinct to prevent his vocal cords from working. A nail jutted up from the floorboards.

James cursed the day he had ever met Shanice. No, he cursed the day he had ever met his ex-wife. If she hadn't been in the picture, then he wouldn't be here, now, wriggling in chocolate dust trying to escape years in prison, all for the theft of some fucking chocolate bars.

The door had one of those fold-down doorstep feet on it, so he grabbed the end of it and pulled it shut, still writhing in pain.

The footsteps had stopped. In front of the door.

32

The rattling and scraping noise shifted to the alleyway entrance. Must be Nia, Edie, or Esme.

The flashlight beam waved above him and then vanished. The footsteps ran toward the back of the warehouse.

A gasp. Then a yelp. He expected Edie or Nia's voice, but he was sure it was Esme's.

"C'mon. Outside," a gruff voice said.

James crawled back into his hiding position. No noise. Not a sound. He stared at the puncture hole in his pants. A little blood, but nothing serious.

A siren wailed as he leaned against the

door. No. Not the cops. They couldn't be taking away Esme.

But there was no mistake about it—two cop cars had arrived. Then plenty of intercom noise, doors opening and closing, and, finally, silence as the two cars drove off.

He glanced down at his phone. Ten percent battery. Of course. No messages, no phone calls.

He texted Shanice. He didn't dare text the others in case the cops had arrested them. The phone did not light up with a magic response. Though he didn't want to waste the battery, he called her. No answer. He shut down the phone to conserve the battery.

Though he had nearly peed his pants while in the storage room, he had held it. But now it was an emergency. A small bathroom stood near the back entrance. That was better. He looked in the mirror and gasped—to say his perfectly coifed hair was disheveled was an understatement. His face was smudged with dirt and chocolate, his clothes were a mess. If he planned to ask for help, he'd better clean up. He took off all his clothes, shook them as best he could, wetted toilet paper and rubbed at the worst stains.

But the cocoa powder had seeped into the material.

No matter, he fixed his hair, put on his clothes back on, and checked his wallet. He had a hundred dollars in cash and all of his cards. Should he call an Uber? But he didn't want to turn on his phone. Maybe he could find a bus.

He blinked in the overcast sunlight as he walked toward the street. An engine roared. He flattened himself against the wall, sure it was the cops. But no one was there.

As he stepped onto the sidewalk, a car screeched and jumped onto the curb in front of him.

James had never been so glad to see a RAV4. The door popped open. He hopped in without confirming it was Shanice.

But it was. She stared straight ahead and hit the accelerator.

They drove to the end of Griffith Street, stopping by a chain-link fence by the bay. Golden-brown scrub surrounded the car, set off against the blue water peeking over the hill.

Shanice turned off the car, turned toward him, and lowered her sunglasses.

"What the fuck, James? Did you tip off the cops?" She shoved her sunglasses back on. "I'm waiting."

"I have no idea what you're talking about—I'm as surprised as you are. Did they get Esme?"

"They sure did."

"Where's everyone else?"

"They escaped as soon as the cops arrived. Nia told me they would come back and pick up Esme—who had come to rescue you."

James gripped the dashboard. "All I know is I went to leave the money as Edie instructed—"

"What money? Edie said nothing about money."

"She said I was to leave it for the chocolate company as compensation."

Shanice sucked air in through her teeth.

"Well, that's what I did. Except a security guard barged in while I was in the office leaving the money. I had to hide in there. Esme must've walked in and surprised the security guard. I heard her voice and then they went outside. Then the cops came. Or at least I heard the sirens. I hid until everyone had gone. That's it, it's the truth."

Shanice set her mouth in a grim line. "Well. We have to rescue Miss Esme now. I've already hired a superb lawyer. At least his rates seem to say that." She sighed. "Everyone else is already at home."

She lowered her sunglasses. "Look me in the eyes, James Bowman." She gestured with two fingers back and forth between them. "Tell me your developer friends have nothing to do with this. You'd better not be a grass, mole, rat, or whatever other low-down trifling scumbag word I can come up with."

"No, ma'am."

"Don't call me ma'am." She started the car. "We'd better get you home soon."

"Why?"

"You seem to always have trouble with your pants. We don't want indecent exposure to be added to our list of criminal charges."

33

———————

Whoops and hollers greeted Shanice and James as they walked through the front door.

"We're all here!" Nia clinked her glass of champagne with Edie's beer bottle.

And there was Miss Esme, sitting on the couch in a beautiful crimson dress, drinking a large scotch. She saluted Shanice and James.

"That was quick." Shanice's eyes widened. "How on earth did you get Miss Esme out so soon?"

"I have the sharpest lawyer in all of California, honey." Esme's fist bounced off the chair arm in triumph. "The best thing is he cleared up the police's missing persons case."

"So your children called the police when you escaped the home?"

Esme gulped down the scotch and turned to Edie. "Either that or the home did itself. My bet is the home did it, not my children. They wouldn't want to be held liable," she said in a quiet voice. Then she pulled up her chin and grinned. "Because I was quite a liability in that home, let me tell you!"

"I don't know what her lawyer did." Nia uncrossed her legs and folded them underneath her. "But we only had to wait twenty minutes outside before Miss Esme walked out."

"He didn't tell me what he said, but all charges were dropped. Looks like I came out better than old Twinkletoes here." Esme pointed at James' pants.

"Hilarious, Miss Esme." James laughed good-naturedly at himself. "I'm going upstairs to shower. I already feel inappropriate standing in front of you like this."

The laughing and chatter grew as he dragged himself up the stairs. Shower or nap first? He'd better shower—he'd never get clean if he fell asleep first. After rummaging around in the bathroom cabinet for painkillers, he found an aspirin bottle shoved in the back.

It slid through his fingers to the floor.

A prescription bottle stared at him from the back of the cabinet. The Vicodin label read "Alana L. Valenti."

He grabbed the Vicodin, opened it, and peered inside, half expecting his ex-wife might be in there. The label said the prescription was from six months ago. She hadn't had any surgery six months ago, so why would she need Vicodin? And how had it ended up in his bathroom cabinet?

The shower steamed up the bathroom, so he padded inside and shut the door. He winced as the hot water coursed over his open wounds, but he didn't take much notice. The prescription bottle occupied his thoughts. As he saw it, there were only two ways the Vicodin could have ended up here. One, his ex had been in the house for some reason—even if she had, why would she leave a prescription behind? It didn't make any sense. The only other reason was that it was put there deliberately. By Shanice. She was the only one who knew about his ex, unless she had told the others. Was this a test? But how was it a test? To make him go crazy? Or what?

The ebbing pain, hot water, and stress made him extraordinarily sleepy. He crawled under the covers.

He dreamt of chocolate, fish, and Vicodin.

———

A POUNDING noise awoke him from his bizarre dreams.

James stared expectantly at the door. No one entered. But the pounding continued.

It was his head. God, he hadn't felt this bad since that night a decade ago with his developer bro-friends. He turned over toward the wall and wriggled under the covers so the sunlight streaming through the blinds would disappear.

Now the pounding at the door was real. Not pounding. Just a sensible knock.

"James?" Shanice cleared her throat. "We let you sleep. Esme, Nia, and Edie are down at the site with the chocolate. We must be there in two hours, so you have forty-five minutes to get ready, K?"

"I never want to see chocolate again." He flung off the covers. "OK. Thanks for letting me sleep in. I needed it. I'll be ready."

He leaned over his legs, holding his head in his hands. That Vicodin would be welcome, but that wouldn't play out well. Someone had thoughtfully placed a bottle of ibuprofen and a water glass next to his bed. After two tablets and a gulp of water, his head stopped swimming.

But his mind kept returning to the Vicodin bottle. It would nag at him all day. He'd have to ask Shanice about it—she'd have to give him an explanation.

After dressing, shaving, and dunking his head into a sink full of cold water five times, he was somewhat ready to face the day.

Shanice sat downstairs, scrolling through her phone. Her usual teacup sat to her side, placed just in front of her plate. She waved a piece of toast at him, but still stared at the screen.

"Morning. You look much better." Then she did a double-take. "Ooo, but your eyes,

James. So bloodshot. That won't do for to-day." She slipped off the stool and padded over to the kitchen cupboard.

James poured himself some coffee and snatched a fresh sesame bagel from the counter. "What a treat. Fresh bagels. Who brought them?"

"Miss Esme rose at five and walked into town." Shanice returned to the kitchen island with a small bottle. "Here. I've got some eyedrops."

"Thanks." He mumbled in between chews on the bagel. Tilting his head backward and inserting the drops, he said, "By the way, do you know why there is a bottle of Vicodin belonging to my ex-wife in the bathroom cabinet?"

When James glanced down again, he saw Shanice gently dabbing her jeans. "I was going to ask you that, actually," said Shanice coolly. "I assumed you needed Vicodin and you used the bottle to carry it in."

James burnt his tongue on his coffee. "Ow. Ah, no. It was definitely not me. I wouldn't carry around something like that to remind me of her."

"No idea. Maybe it fell out of your things when you came and one of the others put it in the bathroom, assuming it was yours?" She looked at her phone and drained her teacup. "Let's go. It's showtime."

34

James blinked.

The mural containers stood on a large strip of brown grass in front of him. That was not surprising. What was surprising was the crowd size at lunchtime on a Monday. The apartment complex loomed up behind them, a sharp gray contrast to the colorful containers below.

Hordes of journalists milled around.

Shanice held James back from the crowd. "Where's everyone? I don't see our crew down there."

"They're inside the containers. Except for Edie. She's with Girard."

His stomach flipped over. He didn't think

he was attracted to her. Perhaps it was disgust.

"Who's handing out the chocolate?"

"Our friends from the apartment complex. They know what to do." Shanice winked at him. "Everything will become clear soon. Before that happens, though, I need an update on the money situation."

"Well, since we just deposited the cash Girard gave us at the bank, Girard texted back he expects everything will go smoothly this morning."

"Smooth is the right word." Shanice chuckled. "So the money is in the bank and I told Girard that. Great. Take a photo of this scene and send it to them."

James did as he was told. "Now what?"

"Now they think everything is going according to plan, so they'll wait for the news stories to roll in."

"Why can't we go down there? Shouldn't we be there?"

Shanice held up a finger as she glanced down at her phone. "Watch this!"

Figures in tight black jumpsuits and balaclavas climbed the container like spiders hatching from an egg sac. They unfurled enormous sheet-banners: *Fulton Girard is corrupt. Developers giving him $. Tisdale Partners-Girard in bed together*. Next to that was an amazingly accurate portrait of Girard and Maxey in bed together. *Gentrifiers go away!* read another sign.

The crowd roared. The TV camera people scurried around like frightened fat quail, trying to get the best angle on the scene. Quinn and another artist James recognized were talking to reporters on microphones.

Shanice smiled. "Great. It's already popping up all over on social media. It will go viral soon. We've used all our connections to make sure."

A few of the black-jumpsuited figures slinked off behind the container into the apartment building.

Shanice blew air through the hands covering her face. "OK, they're safe. They're out of the area. We should get going, too. The cops will show up any minute."

And sure enough, the familiar sound echoed in the distance.

———

"MMM . . . THAT WAS NICE." Edie extracted herself from the octopus-like hands of Fulton Girard. She took a small sip of espresso and smoothed her hand across his chest.

"Why don't we get my things from home and drive up to Napa this afternoon?" he whispered in her ear.

"Sounds like a great idea. But what will you tell Myra?"

"The word 'business trip' is the same as the word 'playtime' in my book." He half growled, half chuckled. "Besides, remember, she left yesterday to visit her sister in the Canary Islands. So it's not like she can walk in on us. Which gives me an idea. How about we spend tonight at my place and drive up to Napa tomorrow? Then we can celebrate properly tonight."

"I love it when your British accent comes out, Mr. Girard," she whispered in his ear. "But what if James sees us? Coincidences happen."

"He'll be too busy with all the publicity for our event this morning." He lifted his phone to Edie's face. "Look at those pictures. Everything's been going smoothly. And here

I was, worried." He moved closer to her. His hand was working its way dangerously up her thigh.

He stiffened. "How did you recognize my British accent?"

She grinned. "Calm down, sweetie. I hear it in your voice. It comes out when you're very relaxed. Or excited."

Fulton's shoulders slumped. "I wasn't entirely honest with you. I was born in England, but we moved to Newark when I was ten."

"Why should you be ashamed of it?"

"I don't know. I got used to hiding it in Newark because kids would make fun of me. So the habit stuck. Besides, with a name like Fulton Girard, you are already the target of a lot of jokes."

"Sounds like your phone is blowing up." Edie looked around. They were ensconced in a cozy corner booth in the empty cafe. "I'll go to the bathroom while you check on your crisis."

His eyes bulged as Edie left. As she turned toward the bathroom, a stream of expletives gushed forth from Mr. Fulton Girard.

She smiled as she swung her bag back and forth, traipsing toward the cafe's back exit. Then she hummed the melody to James Brown's song, *Payback*.

———

"SIR, SIR." The barista with a long ponytail waved at Girard.

"Not now. I'm in the middle of a crisis." He stamped one foot and banged a water glass on the wrought iron table. It shattered into a million pieces.

The barista's lack of reaction made Girard glance up from his phone.

A dirty slob of a man stood next to the barista. His plaid shirt hung half out of his mud-caked jeans. His sparse hair stood on his head.

His gun was pointed at Girard.

"You. You're Fulton Girard, aren't you?"

"Wha—wha—?" He gulped. "That's me." He set down his phone and raised his hands in the air.

"You've been sleeping with my Edie, haven't you, you bastard?"

"What are you blathering about? Who's Edie?"

"Don't lie." The man waved his gun and moved closer to Girard. The barista ran out the front door.

"Set down the gun and we'll talk. I have no idea who this Edie person is. I'm a married man."

"Yeah, I bet you are." The man gave him a crooked smile. "But you're still lying. I watched you two. I've been watching you ever since you set foot in this cafe this morning. I don't know what she's calling herself, but that's Edie, my wife."

"Oh, I uh, I'm married. But yes, I was having an affair—though it hadn't started!" Girard's voice rose and then cracked. "Promise! And I didn't know she was married. She was introduced to me as Evie Lennox by her boyfriend, who works for me, James Bowman."

"James Bowman. What did he look like?" The gun was steady, but slightly lowered now.

"Tall, blond, white guy. Mid-forties. Always stands with his hands on his hips—like this." His arms sat akimbo on his hips.

"Sounds like the guy who came to our house with those other women. And took Edie away from me."

"Other women? What other women?"

"One woman was late thirties or early forties. The other must have been in her twenties. Both Black women."

Girard shook his head. "I think we've been set up. Put the gun down."

The man shook his head and came closer. "If I get wind of you being involved in any way with Edie, those women, or this James-what's-his-face, I'll blow your brains out. OK? See, I don't care about myself. So I'll do anything. In fact, come with me now." He waved Girard out of the cafe with the gun.

Girard began to whimper.

"Follow my directions, asshole."

Girard did as he was told.

35

Abner Maxey leaned over and scooped up the envelope by his front door.

"What's that, dear?" His wife's voice floated in from the hallway.

He chuckled. "So unusual to get letters like this these days, isn't it, Jen?"

"Are you sure it's not dangerous?" Jen stood back in the archway to the hall.

"Nah, it's just a letter. Maybe it's someone who didn't want things traced digitally."

"Why would they be worried about that?"

Abner turned his considerable bulk toward his wife. "No need to worry, hon. I'll come join you for lunch in a minute."

He slid his index finger through the back of the envelope.

"Ow." He sucked on his finger.

One folded sheet was inside. Opening it revealed a jumble of newsprint pasted onto the heavy paper like an old-fashioned ransom note.

"Well, I'll be damned." In disbelief, he read it aloud to himself—not so loud that his wife would overhear, but just loud enough for him to go beyond mouthing the words.

Thanks for all your help, Maxey. We made a great team. Sorry about what comes next.

Don't try to find us, or you'll get yourself in even deeper. We promise.

Love, the Crew.

Jen popped her head in again from the doorway. "Abby, you'd better come. There's something happening you don't want to miss."

Maxey crumpled the letter into a ball and stuffed it into his pocket. He marched into the kitchen to see his wife's laptop open with a large headline reading *The last stand. Developer and Commissioner colluding in gentrification scheme. Statement from Mayor forthcoming soon.*

"They mention your name in the story, Abby. What's it all about?"

But Maxey couldn't answer her. He lay on the floor.

———

GIRARD blinked in the gray sunlight.

The man with the gun walked beside him. "Let's do this nice and easy, OK? See the truck parked over there? You'll get in it and we'll drive away. No heroics."

Girard's knees buckled but he slid into the truck, which was almost as filthy as the man with the gun. Hamburger wrappers, papers, and takeout boxes littered the floor. The truck was parked on a one-way street and Girard's seat faced the street. He eyed the rearview mirror and saw a line of busses approaching. As soon as the first one bore down on them, a few feet behind, Girard opened the passenger door in front of it.

The metal screeching sound was so loud the man with the gun dropped it next to him. Girard scooped it up and hopped out of the car, just before the next bus was about to pass their car. He ran down the street with the gun in his hand, and weaved through the parked cars onto the sidewalk.

He heard the thudding footsteps of someone running from behind him.

"Don't come any closer or I'll shoot."

He snarled and said, "You wouldn't dare."

"Oh no? Try me." Girard suddenly found himself using expressions he had learned from action films.

To the left of him, he saw a figure in a baseball cap whispering into a phone. "Yes. The corner of Pierce and Vallejo. Hurry."

Then the whoop of a siren and flashing lights came into view.

Girard let the gun slip through his fingers onto the sidewalk, turned, and ran. He didn't look back until he had reached Sea Cliff, three hours later.

————

STACKS OF MONEY stood on the table, ready to topple like an eroding cliff into the sea.

Nia settled herself into a seat next to the table. Esme sat across from her, scribbling in a notebook.

"Thanks for keeping this quiet." Nia

cleared her throat. "Xavier, would you make sure the door is locked?"

Xavier, a young person with a matching orange hoodie and hair, jiggled the door. "Locked. We're good."

"OK, so let's run through it once more." Nia jumped out of the chair with the energy of a child who was told they had to sit still.

Pointing to the stacks of money on the table, she continued. "Everyone gets fifty thousand to give to the people we discussed. We'll call those people in a week to make sure they received their fair share."

Xavier crossed their arms. "You don't trust us? We don't need this. It's not supposed to be so fucking transactional."

"Watch your mouth, Xavier," said a hunched-over woman in a wheelchair. "We need all the help we can get."

Xavier smiled but said, "Help? That's what everyone promises us. That's what every one of those fast-talking city people promised. But it was the same thing. Helping us means taking our homes."

Nia sunk back into her chair. "I'm sorry. I'm not very good at this. Shanice is the one who has relationships with you all, but for safety reasons she couldn't be here. All I mean is we're asking to make sure everyone who's supposed to get the money does get it. As we all know, money can make people do things, especially when you don't have enough of it—"

"And more likely when you have too much of it." Esme didn't look up from her phone calculator and scratchpad.

Murmurs of approval went around the room.

"Mhhhh . . . Ms. Esme is right. After everyone gets the money, you all get extra for taking all the risks to make this happen."

"I'm grateful for the money," said a small, wizened man, whose face was covered by a navy baseball cap. "But I also joined up in this thing to make sure we get to keep our homes, right?"

Nia and Esme laughed. "You can bet on that, honey," said Esme. "I just hope it stays this way for a while."

"But it should keep them away for a long time. Both the developers and the city," said Nia. "It'll be too embarrassing for anyone to do anything about it. And we have contacts in the media who will cover the story, should anyone try anything again."

The small figure in the corner nodded approval.

"Let's get started then!" Nia bounced over to the table and scooped up a stack of cash.

Grins all around.

36

The doorknob rattled.

James peeped through the peephole. It was Edie.

"C'mon. Let me in! I forgot my key."

He unlocked the door, opened it. "We were worried. Glad you're here."

"We?" She peered at him suspiciously. "Or do you mean you? Or I should say 'I'?"

"Oh, I, yes, it was me. You're right. The others aren't worried. Or at least they're not showing it." He bowed his head and shuffled his feet.

Edie strode through the door like she was opening a concert for a famous pop star. James trundled after her into the living room, past the pile of suitcases in the hallway.

She threw her head back and waved it as if she were in a shampoo commercial. "Success!" She jumped up and down. "That fucking bastard husband of mine is probably on his way back to Sonoma now, cursing the day he met me."

Shanice leaned back in her chair. "So Sanchez and Malinowsky showed up on time."

"Oh yes. Their cop car showed up right on time. Just as I watched Girard trying to escape Dan."

James plopped down heavily on the sofa. "Sanchez and Malinowsky? Weren't they the port police? And what's this about Dan?"

Shanice sipped her tea and set it down in the middle of the coaster. "We'll explain more once we get out of here, but the short version of the story is one Edie can tell best," she said, surveying Edie, who was glowing in the corner as she munched on a banana.

Her eyes flickered. "Of course." Edie broke off a section of banana and popped it in her mouth. "First, Dan is real. Dan is a bastard, and Dan is my husband. At least until I can divorce the asshole."

"Language, please." Esme continued to scribble numbers on her notepad.

"Sorry, Miss Esme, but really, there aren't any other words to describe him." She draped the banana peel on the side table. "Anyway, Shanice figured out this brilliant way for me to get free of him forever. And to work him into our con at the same time." She smiled at Shanice. "That's the only reason I went along with the honey trap idea. I've never done that and I don't plan on doing it again."

"Looked like you were enjoying yourself." Nia giggled. A banana peel sailed at her head. James thought Edie rather enjoyed it, too. But excellent character actors did get lost in their roles.

Edie shivered. "Girard's not ugly, but his fingers are creepy." She paused and stared out of the window.

"So I called Dan yesterday, since he doesn't know my voice," said Nia. "And I told him if he wanted to see Edie he should show up at Victrola Café."

"And he believed an anonymous phone call?" James shifted in his seat.

"Dan isn't too bright. And he's got such as jealous streak—as you've all witnessed—that any rational thought flies out the window when I'm involved."

"Why did you marry the man?" James glanced at her and then away.

"That's for another day, over heavy drinks." Edie's voice was barely audible.

"Sorry. Please continue."

"So Nia placed the call, and I met Girard at the cafe. I told him we could spend the week in Napa. He didn't need to be told twice. Actually, when I called last night, he said we should go then. But I made him wait, which made him even more desperate. I made out with Girard to provoke Dan. As soon as I saw him outside, watching, I told Girard I had to go to the bathroom, but just walked out the back door. Then I walked around the front and watched the drama unfold."

"And how have you made sure Dan won't bother you? And how will you get a divorce?"

Esme adjusted her reading glasses and coughed. "We, ah, pulled some strings and froze one of his accounts. We couldn't get access to the account, but we could lock it up so he can't get access to it. He'll probably sign those divorce papers now."

"But what's this about Sanchez and Malinowsky—and the police outside the cafe?"

Shanice cleared her throat. "We hired them. They're part of the extended family, if you want to call it that."

"So it means . . ." James rubbed his forehead. "When they rolled up to the container, they were acting, too?"

"Yep," said Shanice.

James glanced at his phone. "Can I have drink? Is it drink time yet? I'm so confused."

Nia twirled around and tapped James on the knee. "Don't worry. You can have all the drinks you want on our plane to Berlin."

37

"Flight 661 to Berlin is delayed by twenty minutes. We appreciate your patience."

People milled about amid the fixed rows of seats. Babies screamed. James was gleeful they would soon be asleep in airplane pods. Alternately nervous and exhausted, he had been drinking a steady stream of coffee since they left the house. Probably not the best idea, but he couldn't stop. He jiggled his leg.

"This may be a stupid question, but why are we going to Berlin?" asked James.

The corner of Shanice's mouth lifted in a grin. "They'll never think to search for us there. It's a diversion."

James opened his mouth and closed it.

He now knew better than to ask where they'd be going next. His leg stopped jiggling and he leaned back, arms behind his head. He pushed away the caffeine-induced jitters and relaxed.

"Looks like you've let go a little." Shanice smiled.

He sighed. "Yes. Better to trust the plan, right?"

Esme made a clicking noise with her tongue. "You've got it. Trust Shanice."

Nia rolled her neck. "I'll pay for one of those massage chairs around the corner. I can't sit here."

"I'll watch your stuff." Shanice whispered, "I think she's a nervous flyer. Kind of like me."

Esme was glued to her phone. "Look." She showed the phone to Shanice and James.

Shanice took the phone and held it up so James could see. The headline read *Prominent developer dies of heart attack. Police investigation.* "Poor Maxey. He did help us out."

James nodded slowly. "Yes, he did, but do you mean something else?"

"The word 'double-crossed' sounds so

old school, but there isn't a better word for it." Shanice sipped her green tea. "That's what we did with Maxey. Originally, I thought he'd be the mark, but then when Girard came along, he was too good to pass up. Besides, developers with Maxey's politics are a dime a dozen—hell, it's what developers do, anyway. But Girard? I couldn't pass up the opportunity to force him to glance in the mirror. So I devised a way Maxey would lose out on the deal, too, but Girard was the prime target."

"So you're saying you made Maxey think he was in on screwing over Girard, when in fact he did that—plus being screwed over himself?"

"Mhhh . . . though I am sorry about his heart attack. I don't want anyone to die. But if it was a result of our news, well, it was only a matter of time before he had other news that caused a heart attack."

"The police are investigating."

Shanice smiled. "Well, I did leave him a note."

"Why did you leave him a note?"

"I did feel we owed him some sort of explanation."

Edie arrived with smoothies in a tray. "Green Goddess for Shanice, Plum Passion for Miss Esme, and Pink Pastel for James." She handed out the drinks, one by one.

"I didn't order pink pastel." James huffed. "I ordered strawberry banana raspberry."

Edie laughed. "It's called a Pink Pastel. I can't help it."

The cool sludge of the smoothie slid down his throat.

James smiled. "Thanks. I needed it. By the way, what did you do with Opal?"

"Left her with my mom."

Esme turned to Edie, nodding her head in apparent approval. "Shanice's telling James how Maxey was involved." Edie nodded as she sucked on her straw.

"We heard Maxey wanted to buy Juniper Downs. Rumors swirled the residents would be forced out, so we researched it. He planned to buy the property. So we told him about a scheme to get what he wanted—the same you told Girard, with one major differ-ence. The difference was Maxey hoodwinked Girard himself."

Edie set down her smoothie. "Maxey was kind of our outside man. I mean, he wasn't really the convincer, but his job was to influence Girard."

"Yep. We knew Maxey had been involved in shady backroom deals in the past. We figured if we approached this game straight up—as it appeared to you, James—then he would get really suspicious."

"That's why Shanice is such a genius," said Esme. "She realized Maxey's weakness. It wasn't greed. It was a type of power, but not the kind we associate with developers, necessarily."

Shanice nodded. "He psychologically needed to have the upper hand. We knew if he thought he was getting one over on Girard—even though from his perspective Girard didn't lose anything—then he'd be game."

"OK, so Maxey went along because of greed and because he got one over on another powerful man?"

Three heads nodded.

James ran his hands through his hair. "Brilliant. Though now the police are investigating."

"What are they going to find? Nothing. If they find anything, it'll implicate Girard.

And Girard will do anything to keep the scandal hush-hush. Though it's a little too late for him."

James was about to ask her about the supposed plan for revenge on his ex, but Nia was running toward them.

38

Nia leaned over them. "Cops."

"Quick." Shanice leapt up. "Run to the bathrooms. I'll text you, James, when it's safe to come out."

Esme was the first into the bathroom. The woman moved quickly. Was she really that old?

James lounged in the entry to the men's bathroom, watching. He decided he would go into the stall if the police came toward the bathroom.

They were definitely San Francisco police, not TSA or other airport security. His mouth went dry as he watched them march up to the counter for the two Lufthansa flights, but he somehow remained casually propped up against the wall.

One cop talked to the employee at the Flight 661 counter, while the other spoke to the one at Flight 325, bound for Frankfurt. They showed the airline employees their phones, presumably photos of whomever they were looking for.

The Lufthansa employee at the counter switched on the intercom. "Flight 661 will begin preboarding for those passengers who need extra time, as well as those traveling with small children."

The cop still stood at the counter. Waiting.

Families with children and some elderly passengers made their way to the front.

"Flight 661 will now board those traveling in our premium class."

Time to board.

He glanced down at his phone. No texts.

When he looked up, he saw one cop moving toward the bathroom. Most likely the men's bathroom.

James rolled his suitcase into the stall and stood, waiting.

He peered underneath the gap in the

door. Two black shoes in black pants stood there. Not in front of the urinals. And not in front of the sink.

They just stood there.

Though he did not believe in God, or at least not enough to pray in non-stressful situations, he stared at the ceiling and prayed.

Knock. Knock.

"Sir. Would you come out, please? Police."

"Ah, OK." James made shuffling noises and then flushed the toilet.

He opened the door.

A small officer with dark hair and a rigid posture stood in front of him. "We're searching for a few individuals, sir. May I see your passport?"

"Why my passport? Why not just ID?"

"Because we're in the international terminal, sir. You shouldn't be here without a passport."

"Mind if I wash my hands first?"

The cop scowled but gave him a slow nod.

Where had he put the passports Shanice had given him? He remembered. In the front pocket of his suitcase.

He made an elaborate show of drying his hands and then unzipped the suitcase. Nothing was inside.

"Ah, Officer. I had it a minute ago."

The cop sighed. "What's your name, sir?"

"James Vanderlin."

"Vanderlin, sir?"

"Yes, something wrong with the name, officer? It's Dutch."

"Well, Mr. Vanderlin, we need to find that passport."

James took off his jacket and riffled through the pockets. Finally. Success! Thank God it was James Vanderlin's passport and not James Ambrose's passport. Though he much preferred Ambrose.

"We'll now board all passengers for Flight 661 with nonstop service to Berlin. Please make your way to the counter," drawled the intercom.

The cop flipped through the passport, turning it up and down and around as if he couldn't read.

James held his shoulders back, tilted his nose upward, and let out an exasperated sigh. He'd finally internalized what Shanice had told him a few months ago. One night, when he had become a nervous wreck about, well, everything, she'd said, "People in charge can smell fear. As soon as you let them know you're nervous, they've got the upper hand." Then she showed him the explicit gestures of confidence he should use in a situation like this. He hadn't consciously used them until now.

"Well, Mr. Vanderlin," the officer said, with extra emphasis on 'Vanderlin', "Looks like you can go. If I were you, I'd stay in Berlin for a while."

"Don't worry. I plan to." James threw back his head as he marched out of the bathroom.

———

"WHAT ARE YOU DOING IN HERE?" A woman stood near the sink with her hands on her hips.

"Oh, sorry. Wrong side." James scurried out of the women's bathroom before the irate woman could follow him. Too late, he thought it would have been better to ask her about a gender-neutral bathroom.

No sign of his crew.

One straggler stood at the counter, waiting for their ticket to be validated.

And that person wasn't a member of the crew.

He glanced at his phone again. No texts. Should he get on the plane?

A flight attendant held up her index finger. "Sir, we're closing the gates for boarding."

"Yes. I want to ensure my friends boarded the plane. Four women, one elderly, one in her twenties?"

She sucked in air through her teeth. "Sorry, sir. My colleague was helping me, so I'm not sure. Besides, it's confidential information."

"Yes, well, I'll have to hope they're on the plane, won't I?" He handed her the ticket. "What was all the fuss with the police?"

"They're searching for a group of women. Strange that you are, too." She said it more to herself than to James.

Before she could made any more comments, he dashed down the makeshift corridor to the plane.

As he made his way down the aisle past a few sleeping pods, he heard clapping.

Nia made a whooping sound. "You made it, James!" She raised a glass of champagne.

3C. He shoved his suitcase in the overhead compartment and slumped into the pod next to Shanice. Edie and Esme were already watching films, and Nia was engaged in an elaborate stretching routine—in between sips of champagne, of course.

Even though he had known Shanice a relatively short but intense amount of time, he had never seen her so relaxed. Her legs were propped up and she was wriggling her toes in her special Lufthansa socks.

She held up a plate of fruit in salute. "You made it, James. In more ways than one. Congratulations, you passed the last test."

Shanice aimed a grape at his mouth. James opened and she lobbed it in.

"Ladies and gentlemen, we'll prepare for takeoff shortly. Flying time to Berlin is ten hours and fifteen minutes."

39

"So, are you going to tell me all the tests I passed?" James turned to her after they had leveled off at cruising altitude.

"It's as good a time as any. Where should I begin?"

"Can you start with all the things I didn't know about? I know about Maxey. What about Girard?"

"Oh, we definitely set you up with the Girard scenario."

James gripped his armrest. "Wait. Let me guess. Maggie Lambert was somehow connected to all of this."

Shanice shook her empty glass, still filled with ice, at him. "Bravo. You knew something wasn't right about Maggie, didn't you?"

"That day at the party—when she just happened to be drunk and interrupt our conversation? It seemed too staged."

"Well done. Right you are. But it's probably not what you think." She slid the glass around in a circle on her tray. "There must be some loose ends you can connect to her. Or at least try to connect to her."

James leaned back and closed his eyes. The scrap of paper Edie found in Myra's bag at the ballet. The stolen paintings from the Girards' home during the party. Why hadn't he heard a fuss about that from Girard himself? Esme's computer scheme. The BMW that followed them.

He jerked his head up so quickly he winced from the whiplash. "Maggie stole the paintings. She followed us in the BMW."

"But what about Myra's scrap of paper?"

James rubbed his jaw.

"Here. Read this text I received before we took off." Shanice handed James her phone.

We did it! Off to Madagascar with Maggie. XO MG

"Who is MG?"

Shanice began to roll her eyes and then stopped. "I'm sorry, James. It's so much fun to torture you a bit. It's a new experience for me." She smiled. "MG is Myra Girard."

"Myra?" James leaned back again as turbulence hit the plane.

Shanice gripped her armrests and closed her eyes.

"It helps to imagine we're on a boat. The turbulence is like water. Not pleasant in a storm, but not life-threatening, either."

Shanice sighed. "Thanks. Not a big fan of flying." Now the plane flew smoothly, except for occasional bumps. She rolled her head toward him while it was on the headrest. "Myra Girard knew her husband was a liar and a cheat of the worst sort. She had apparently tried to leave him a number of times, but was stopped by the risk of losing her comfortable lifestyle. She met Maggie soon after she and Girard had moved to San Francisco. They fell in love. That's probably what made her go through with it."

"How did you meet Myra?"

"At a gallery opening. A San Francisco art opening is always packed with marks. Myra had too much to drink and spilled out her life story—and her champagne—on me. I was sympathetic, of course. At first I thought she might be the mark, but then when I realized she had such a bastard for a husband, my view shifted. She became our ally."

"Wasn't it a little risky?"

"No plan is without risk. Besides, I only told her what she needed to know on her end. She didn't need to know about the development plans. She was completely wrapped up in her own little world."

"So why did she have a slip of paper with my name on it—the one Edie found at the ballet?"

"Amateur mistake. She must have been taking notes when she was talking to me and left the paper in her bag. Edie found it by accident."

"And the paintings? And Esme's computer shenanigans?"

"Maggie or Myra stole the paintings. Probably together. I have a feeling Myra must have made some excuse about loaning them or something else. They sold them immediately to fund their travels. As for Esme's computer files, Myra needed all of the financial statements from Girard—he kept a tight hold on them—so she could access the funds. She was hopeless with computers, so Esme did it for her."

"Clever." He sighed.

Shanice peered at him. "What is it?"

James pursed his lips. "I never believed your explanation of why Alana's Vicodin prescription was in the bathroom cabinet. Did you lie to me?"

Shanice sat up and gazed into his eyes. "Yes. I did. I know it seems cruel, but I needed to see how you'd react if you were confronted with her name out of context. It was right before we finished everything, and I needed to know you could be trusted. Please forgive me."

He gritted his teeth. "I can forgive that, but I can't forgive your failed promise for revenge on Alana. I've been a good sport the whole time—"

"You have. And you've changed."

"How so?"

"For the better. Notice how much more relaxed you were in the airport, despite having drunk ten gallons of coffee?"

He smiled. "You're right, but don't distract me. Tell me about Alana. I know you wouldn't forget your promise to me, so what happened?"

Shanice rattled the ice in her glass meditatively. "I was going to wait until we landed to let you make a decision, but I can see I'm not going to have any peace until I tell you."

James crossed his arms. "Damn right."

"Believe it or not, I went round and round in circles about the plan to get revenge on Alana."

"You? I can't believe it. You have everything planned out five steps in advance."

Shanice sighed. "I try to make it look easy because it's hard for me to trust anyone . . . But that's a story for another time. The point is I couldn't figure out a way to make the plan work when Maxey, Girard, and Alana—as well as her lover, Seth—all traveled in the same circles. There were too many risks that people would gossip to each other. Or somehow find out about your past history."

"So you're saying we managed to get revenge on Edie's husband, help your aunt, and bring Nia and Esme along for the ride and the cash, but you couldn't help me?"

"When you say it like that, doesn't it sound a little childish?"

He wasn't going to back down. "I'll admit it's a lot to ask, but you're a magician."

A slow grin spread across her face. "I wouldn't say I'm a magician. I just have a lot of experience. In any case, you can have your revenge."

"What do you mean *have*?"

Shanice pulled out her phone and clicked through to her photos. She gave the phone to James.

Seth Hummel, Mr. Sunglasses, stared back at him. "This is the photo you showed to your aunt at Juniper Downs, right?"

"Didn't you wonder why I did that?"

"Yes. I assumed it was part of the plan."

"But then you never asked about it again."

"I didn't want to bother you. Besides, things were moving so fast."

"Well, I showed it to Auntie Didi for a reason. See, I have a friend on the ethics commission. If there was any evidence Seth Hummel was pressuring Juniper Downs tenants about problems with the buildings, my friend will want to know about it. And she doesn't play. Seth Hummel will be before a judge before you know it. Especially if there's evidence he was tampering with the buildings to make them unsafe."

"What do you mean? Was he doing that?"

Shanice shook her head. "No, though I wouldn't put it past him given what I've heard through the grapevine." She turned and looked James in the eyes. "All you have to do is give me the word and I'll send an email to my friend as soon as we arrive in Berlin. You won't get revenge on Alana directly. But because the two of them are now married, she'll be dragged through the courts, too."

James leaned back and closed his eyes. He still wanted to revenge . . . didn't he? Maybe, but not this way. He had a new life now, or at least some money and some friends.

"I don't know, Shanice. I didn't want revenge this way."

"Oh? And what had you imagined? That we'd murder Seth and Alana? Or what?"

He rubbed the bridge of his nose. "I don't know what I thought. I did have murderous intent, yes, but I couldn't really go through with it."

"All you have to do is tell me and I'll send that email. You don't have to do anything more."

The corners of Shanice's eyes scrunched up.

"Are you daring me to say yes?"

"I am."

"I can't do it. I can't do it, dammit."

Shanice raised her glass. "Congratulations, James, you're officially a grifter with a conscience. Welcome to the crew."

She looked at her watch. "And it's about time we found another mark."

The End

Did you enjoy this book? If so, I'd appreciate a quick review on Amazon. Thank you!

ENJOYED GRIFT?

I rely on you, dear reader, to help me spread the word about my books. If you enjoyed the book, a thoughtful review on Amazon will help other readers find *Grift*. You can leave a review here. Thank you!

If you'd like discounts and updates on new releases, you can join my reader group here.

rl@rldonovanauthor.com

ABOUT THE AUTHOR

RL Donovan loves mysteries, thrillers, capers, and puzzles—anything with a twist. As a former academic, RL uses the unbelievable but true escapades of her colleagues and students to create absurd scenarios for her books.

rl@rldonovanauthor.com